STARLIGHT

Other titles from Geoffrey Lewis:

Flashback
ISBN 0-9545624-0-2

Strangers
ISBN 0-9545624-1-0

Winter's Tale
ISBN 0-9545624-2-9

Cycle
ISBN 0-9545624-3-7

ABOUT THE AUTHOR

Geoffrey Lewis was born in Oxford, in 1947. Educated at the City's High School, and Hatfield University (then a polytechnic), he has since followed a varied career, including spells as a research chemist, security guard, and professional photographer. After many years in the motor trade, and eight years as captain of a canal-based passenger boat, he is now semi-retired, and concentrating upon his writing.

Photographer, bell-ringer, beer-drinker, and American car enthusiast, he lives in a narrowboat on the Grand Union Canal, where he has written his five published books, including four in the popular detective series featuring Detective Inspector David Russell.

STARLIGHT

Geoffrey Lewis

SGM
Publishing

ISBN 0-9545624-5-3

Printed in Great Britain
by CPI Bath

First published in Great Britain in 2005 by

SGM Publishing
Cosgrove Wharf, Lock Lane, Cosgrove, Northants MK19 7JR
info@sgmpublishing.co.uk
www.sgmpublishing.co.uk

For Robin
In celebration of fifty years of friendship.

Acknowledgements

It may seem unusual to include a list of acknowledgements in a work of fiction, but this time it is only too appropriate. A boater myself of many years standing, I wanted to be sure that the background to this story was believable and accurate – published sources I have used to this end included Alan Faulkner's booklet *Willow Wren,* and *Our Canal in Oxford* by Mark Davies and Catherine Robinson. Tom Foxon's book *No. 1*, his memoir of the days when he was working the 'Oxford Cut' in the 1950s, was also invaluable.

My personal thanks go to Brian Collings, an old friend and the man who taught me my boating skills, such as they are. A man who knew the canals in their working days, and a personal friend of Joe and Rose Skinner, his reminiscences added much to my ability to write this novel. Also my thanks to Tom Foxon himself, for his approval of the project and his permission to include him as a character in my story.

And on the jacket: My thanks to my friends Aran Gardner and Kynan Parris-Jones for being 'Harry Turner' and 'Jake Woodrow' for the front cover, and to Tom 'Mac' MacManus for being an older 'Harry' for the back cover. Photography by myself!

Last, but by no means least, my thanks as always to Roger Wickham of Amherst Publishing, who does all the hard work of turning my writing into actual books!

Geoffrey Lewis

Preamble

I live here now.

Things have changed over the years, at Burdon Lock – I have mains electricity now, a television set, DVD player, washing machine and drier, a fridge-freezer, even a microwave oven, although I don't use that much. And I have gas for my cooking, even if it is delivered by a man with a big tanker who backs carefully down my lane and connects his long black umbilical to a tank discretely hidden behind the hedge. Inside, the rooms are much as I remember them, although brightened up and rearranged many times over by the different owners. The old Victorian fireplace and mantle are still there in the living room; now, in pride of place at the centre of the mantleshelf, stands a beautiful hand-made model of an old working boat…

Perhaps it was blind chance, that led me back to live in the place of my childhood's greatest happiness, and its greatest sorrow. But, although I am not a religious man, I do believe that there is some kind of outside influence, a power which can and does guide our faltering steps through the journey of life: So – was it chance, or destiny, which led me to make that rare visit to the village, to that meeting outside the long-closed post office with old

Mabel Caddick? I remember her as an energetic, cheerful housewife in her thirties; she's over eighty, now. In the course of conversation, she asked, did I know that the old lock cottage was up for sale? I hadn't known – but I made it my business to find out, to contact the agent for the details; and to persuade Mary that this really was the place where we wanted to live, now that Sarah, our youngest, was ready to fly the nest.

We got it at a good price, too. Houses in the middle of nowhere, still more than a mile from the nearest vestiges of civilisation, probably aren't too easy to sell, even if one of the previous owners had laid in a proper crushed-stone roadway, and converted the larger of Ernie Woodrow's old store sheds into a two-car garage. Not that I need two cars now, of course, not since my Mary's been gone. We had almost six years here, together. The children keep on at me to move, to go and live with one of them, or at least to buy myself a little place somewhere else – they're afraid the memories will get to me, I suppose, the thought of her short, hard struggle against that final illness; or the being alone here, where we'd had so many happy times in those last years. But I still love it here; I like to meet, chat with, the people who come through the lock – all holiday-makers, now, of course. The likes of old Joe Skinner, Frank Shine, Albert Beechey and the rest are long gone. And sometimes, of an evening, I let the starlight on the still water take me back to those days of my childhood…

It isn't just Mary. The kids don't talk about that, but I know it's in their minds, all the same. But then, that's the reason I've decided to write this, to set down in my own words the story of that eventful time, the spring and summer of the year we moved out of Oxford, to live in the village, when I discovered the countryside, the canal, and so much more. And if I'm going to write it, I suppose I'd better get on with it…

Henry Turner
September 2004

Chapter One

'Come on, Harry, give it a chance, you'll love it there, you wait and see!'

It wasn't that my father was an insensitive man, far from it. But by then he was in his late forties; he'd been running, expanding, the small engineering firm his father had started in Kidlington, for almost twenty-five years, and he'd forgotten what it was like to be eleven years old. He'd forgotten how small your world is at that age, a world which consists of family, school and friends – and now, he and my mother were proposing to cut me off from two of those three things, at a stroke, and without a thought for my feelings. Or at least, that was how it seemed to me:

'But Dad – I won't be able to see Nicky, or Max, or anyone!'

He put a comforting hand on my shoulder, gave me one of his easy smiles:

'Don't worry, Harry – once we get settled in, we can go back to Oxford to see them; or maybe you could have them over to stay, from time to time? And anyway, you'll soon make new friends, you'll see, especially once you start school again after the holiday!'

His cheerful words weren't convincing – he meant what he said, I know, but I also knew from experience that his good intentions often disappeared under the weight of business. And the thought of having to start at another new school, after just two terms at St Peter's College, depressed me even more. I wouldn't miss St Peter's, to be honest – I'd gone there having easily passed my eleven-plus exam, but the snobbish atmosphere and level of teasing, which just stopped short of real bullying, hadn't endeared the place to me. But would my new school be any better? Or could it, horror of horrors, be even worse? I was to start at the County High School, in Banbury, at the end of the Easter holiday – we were moving then, so as to minimise the disruption to my education. Or rather to *cause* it, from my schoolboy point of view.

Looking back, I can now, I think, understand my parent's eagerness to move. Home, the only home I'd ever known, had been a big three-story town house on the Woodstock Road, in North Oxford. A cavernous, dark, echoey place, but wonderful for a kid, with so much space to play in, to chase around in with my friends – and so many places to get away into, to avoid chastisement for some misdemeanour, or to keep out of my father's eye on the not-very-frequent occasions when problems at work put him in a bad mood. Things I learnt later, comments my mother made when I was much older, led me to understand that they had hoped and planned for a large family; but, for reasons she never disclosed, that hadn't proved possible. After several miscarriages, I was their first-born; and she did tell me once that, after my birth, the doctors had advised them not have any more children. It's my belief that the big house had been intended for the four or five kids to grow up in, and the move to the cottage in Burdon

Leigh was a final acknowledgement that I was going to be an only child, whatever their hopes might have been. The only question that remains in my mind is why did they wait so long? An earlier move would have been easier for me, and, I would have thought, for them.

Be that as it may, we moved that March, in 1955, when I was eleven years old. The cottage – Old Bakery Cottage, in Church Lane – was still, by the standards of the day and the locality, quite a big house. The original cottage hadn't been, but the last owner had had the bakery buildings, attached to the rear of what had been the kitchen, converted to expand the living space, so now there was a huge single-story kitchen at the back, where the old ovens had been, a dining room next to that in the old mixing room with an extra bedroom above, and, remarkably for the time, in such a rural setting, an indoor toilet and bathroom, a the top of the stairs. It came as a real shock to a townie boy like me to discover that many of our neighbours still had to take a trek down the garden to relieve themselves, and bath in an iron tub in front of the fire!

Burdon Leigh is, even now, a very small place – in those days, it was positively tiny. There were a number of outlying farms, but the village itself consisted of three straggly streets, which met at the green, across which the church and pub faced each other like old adversaries drawing breath for the next round, with the little shop and post office standing like a diminutive referee off to one side. Old Bakery Cottage lay at the far end of Church Lane, all of eight doors away from the green – one of the farmhouses stood a few hundred yards further on, effectively marking the Northern extremity of the village.

We moved in during Holy Week, a fact which drew a few disapproving stares from the more old-fashioned residents when we all turned up in church on Easter Morning. But most of the locals were very welcoming; indeed, it took all my mother's diplomatic skills to get us away in time for her to cook the Sunday dinner! I was feeling pretty lonely – scouting the pews for any likely boys my own age, who might prove to be future play-mates, hadn't been very fruitful. There were a couple of girls – but, at eleven years old, no-one wants to play with *girls!* The only boys were much younger than me, so my father's assurance of making new friends was beginning to sound rather hollow.

I spent the last few days of that holiday pretty much alone. Dad was at work, of course, but my mother was at home with me – she, like many married women of those days, was an old-fashioned, non-working housewife. She and I explored the village itself together, talking to the local people whenever the chance arose, but I soon got bored with listening to her chatting with every housewife we met. A lot of the time, I would go off on my own, wandering beyond the bounds of Burdon Leigh into the open countryside, along the narrow lanes or across the fields – I soon learnt to stick to the marked footpaths and bridleways, after being roundly told off by more than one cheerfully angry farmer! There was one such path, leading away from Church Lane next to the farmhouse, along from our cottage – I was stood there, contemplating exploring it one day, when the farmer's daughter, a girl of about thirteen, came past with one of her horsy friends, and warned me against it:

'You don't want to go down *there,* there're nasty, dirty boatees live down *there!'* They sniggered at my startled, uncomprehending expression and hurried away; but, unsure of the validity or otherwise of their words, I decided to give that way a miss – at least, until another day, maybe. By the end of the holidays, I was beginning to know my way around the area – or, I thought I did.

Chapter Two

A Tuesday morning in early April, and my first day at my new school. A special bus was laid on for us kids who lived in the outlying villages; Burdon Leigh was its last-but-one pick-up before running in to Banbury, and we waited for it on the village green.

'We' consisted of the two younger boys I'd noticed in church, the farmer's daughter and her giggly friend, and one other boy, several years older than me. The last wore the same maroon-and-black uniform as I did, his looking a little worn by comparison with mine, pristine in its newness; the girls were on their way to the town's secondary modern school, and the younger lads to a primary school in the last village we passed on our way. Observing this mixed collection, I thought again that the possibility of me making new friends here was pretty remote.

I stood there, feeling rather conspicuous – the two girls were passing whispered comments, and giggling, and I couldn't help the idea that they were talking about me; the older boy, who I knew to be the son of the couple who ran the Post Office, studiously ignored me. Only the little kids spoke; one of them asked who I was, and I responded with my name, told them we'd moved into the Old Bakery; they replied in kind, but I didn't take a lot of notice of what they said, to be honest. They must have been about seven or eight – much too young to come within the sphere of someone of my advanced years.

And then the school bus arrived, swinging around the green and grinding to a halt in front of us; at the same time, I became aware of someone hurrying up behind us, from the direction in which I had come. As I went to climb the steps into the bus, I glanced back, to see a boy of about my own age, also in the maroon and black of the County High – he looked rather dishevelled, and he was panting, as if he'd been running. I sat in a vacant seat near the front; the older boy went past me to sit a row or two further back, and the two little kids hustled off to join some of their mates who were occupying the back row of seats. The newcomer climbed the steps, and paused to give me an appraising glance before also passing me, to sit somewhere near the back. I had a quick impression of a tanned face, a mop of thick light brown hair, and eyes that were a bright, startling blue.

In Banbury, after dropping the chattering group of youngsters at their village primary school, we all dismounted. The girls all trooped off along the road to their school, and the dozen or so of us boys destined for the County strolled with varying degrees of enthusiasm through the gates. I was by now feeling very nervous – it had been one thing to start at a new school the previous autumn, when all of my class had been equally disoriented, but to start now, as a new boy coming into the midst of a settled group, left me wishing I was somewhere, anywhere, else.

Then a voice spoke behind me: 'You're the new kid, from the Bakery, aren't you?'

I turned, to see the boy who'd been running for the bus; I smiled tentatively, and replied: 'Yes – I'm Harry Turner. It's my first day here.'

He gave me the ghost of a smile, but stuck out his hand: 'Jake Woodrow – How'd yer do? Which class are you in?'

I took the proffered hand, shook it formally, replied as I had been taught: 'Fine, thanks – how are you? I don't know, yet – I've got to report to the Headmaster's office, I suppose he'll tell me.'

Jake nodded as he released my hand: 'Oh, right. Maybe I'll see you later.' His tone was oddly flat, as if the prospect held little concern for him; he went on: 'Turn left inside the main door – The Wombat lives in the office at the end.' He turned and strolled off, presumably towards his own class; I went in through the tall, imposing doors of the main building, and followed his directions.

After a brief pep talk by Mr Wanstone, his secretary, a plump, cheerful woman with spectacles and greying hair, led me along the maze of corridors until she knocked at a door, opening it at the resounding 'come' from within. She ushered me inside:

'This is Mr Atkinson, he'll be your form-master, Turner. Mr Atkinson – Henry Turner.' Atkinson was a shortish, heavily built man with a florid face, his hairline receding from a high forehead and turning to a steely grey as it did so; he was dressed, as I came to know was his habit, in a rather loudly-checked sports jacket and dark trousers.

His voice, as he beckoned me forward, was as loud as the jacket:

'Come here, boy, let's see you, then!' He looked me up

and down: 'Hmm – Turner, Henry Turner. Is that what they call you?'

'M-most people call me Harry, sir.'

'People?'

'My p-parents, sir. And my – and my friends.' What friends? I thought, as I said this. He surprised me by clapping me on the back:

'Harry it is, then! But we're a bit more formal around here, Harry; we usually call people by their surnames, in school. So you'll just be Turner, most of the time, right? Now, find yourself an empty desk, and take a seat while I go over your new timetable for this term.'

I looked around. The desks were all double units – there were a few spare seats, a couple near the back of the room, and one, at the right-hand end of the second row. The occupant of its pair was the boy who'd introduced himself on the steps outside; I made my way across there, and took the chair beside him, giving him a smile as I did so. He looked up; his echoing smile looked a little surprised.

The format then was that we had seven lessons in the day – two before morning break, two after, and three more after lunch. That first day, the first lesson was taken up with Mr Atkinson reeling off the timetable while we all scribbled it down in the front of our form notebooks, and then his rather prolonged observations on the particular areas which each of the boys needed to concentrate upon in order to improve their intellectual standing – being the new boy did have that consolation at least; he had no embarrassing comments for me!

Another advantage of being in a group familiar with

their surroundings became apparent as we headed for the next class – the others all knew the way around, so I had only to follow! First day at St Peter's had been utter chaos, with two entire first-year forms milling around, for a large part of the time completely lost. I had little chance to talk to my companion that morning, even though I found myself sitting next to him in another of the classrooms we visited; at break, he disappeared somewhere, only returning in time to join the rest of the form in the History room. At lunch, too, he vanished outside while I joined most of the school in the refectory.

School dinners then were just as depressing as the comedians would have you believe. Half an hour later, feeling full but unsatisfied by the tasteless stodge I had eaten, I wandered out into the tarmac-surfaced playground area. I had been engaged in some desultory conversation with a few of my class-mates, facing their innocent but irritating curiosity about their new fellow, but had not so far struck up any, even preliminary, friendships. Looking around, I spotted Jake Woodrow sitting on top of a low raised concrete structure, just along from the main door I had emerged from; I walked up to him and asked: 'Do you mind if I join you?'

He looked up; after a moment, he waved a disparaging hand: 'If you want to.'

I climbed up, took a seat beside him; he sat back, his arms akimbo, hands clasped behind his head, shoulders resting against the stone wall behind him. After wriggling about to get comfortable, I tried echoing his pose, and found it quite restful; we sat there, elbows raised, legs stretched out, ankles crossed. Neither of us spoke again for a while – he didn't seem inclined to conversation, and I was lost for something to say.

But at last, just as I began to feel the silenced becoming embarrassing, a question occurred to me: 'You live near me, in Burdon Leigh, do you?'

His reply was hardly informative: 'Not exactly.'

I tried again: 'You came from my direction, didn't you, this morning?'

'Yes, I suppose so. We live outside the village.'

'Is that why you'd been running, to catch the bus?'

'Who said I'd been running?'

'You were panting, so I thought…'

He looked around at me, and at last his face relaxed into a faint smile: 'Yeah, okay, I was a bit late. My Dad'd give me hell if I missed school, so I had to run rather than miss the bus.'

'Oh, I see.' I was running short of conversation, but, rather to my surprise, he took it up: 'Your father's an engineer, isn't he?'

'That's right – he's got his own workshop, in Kidlington.'

'Big place, is it?'

'Quite big – he's got a couple of dozen men working for him, now.'

'Oh.' He sounded impressed, but I detected a hint of disappointment in his tone, which puzzled me. Then he asked a question I didn't understand: 'Is it near the cut?'

'The what?' He looked around again, and the look of disappointment was clear in his face: 'Never mind!'

The next moment he got up and slid down from the platform: 'I'm going for a pee – see you later.' Once again, his tone was uninterested. I stared after him, wondering how I'd annoyed him, as he strolled across the playground to the toilet block at the far side.

I slid forward, to sit on the edge of the concrete dais, despairing of ever making any friends in this inhospitable place. But then, two of my other class-mates walked up, boys I had spoken to briefly over the dinner table; I knew them only as Pocock and Smith. The latter, a short, heavily-built kid with freckles and sandy hair, was the one who spoke to me now:

'Turner – can we give you a bit of advice?'

'Of course, thank you.'

'You should be careful who you make friends with, here, Turner. I mean, some of the boys here are, shall we say a bit undesirable, you understand?'

I wasn't sure what to make of this: 'How do you mean, Smith?'

He gave me a self-satisfied smile: 'Well – my father is the manager of the Banbury branch of the Oxford United Bank; Pocock's family owns one of the biggest shops in the town. *Woodrow's* father is a lock-keeper on the canal. Now do you understand?'

The words had been spoken in a tone of utter disparagement, but the idea enthralled me: 'He *is?*' I couldn't keep the interest out of my voice.

Smith and his friend gave me looks verging on disgust: 'Your father runs his own business, doesn't he, Turner?'

'Yes, he does!'

'So, that makes you one of *us,* doesn't it? *His* family are dirty boatees!'

I was beginning to feel quite angry. The boy's attempt

to persuade me not to talk to Jake Woodrow, for that was clearly his aim, annoyed me not because, at that time, I had any on-going desire to do so, but because of its intention to interfere with my own freedom of choice in the matter. Now, I got on my high horse:

'I think I'm entitled to make up my own mind about who I choose to talk to, here or anywhere else! Thank you for your advice – but *I'll* decide whether to follow it, or not!' I jumped to the ground, and stalked off.

* * *

During that afternoon, I found empty seats next to Jake in two more of our lessons. Out of spite for Smith and his mate, I took them both times, amused by the look of annoyance on their faces when they saw. By the end of the day, it had occurred to me that their influence could well be the reason for those empty seats – or did the other boys all feel the same way? Either way, I was beginning to have a degree of sympathy for the stocky kid with the bright blue eyes and self-reliant manner.

Chapter Three

During those afternoon lessons when I was sat beside him, Jake still spoke hardly at all. In his silence, I sensed a kind of wariness which at the time I didn't understand. Nor did I entirely understand the obvious antipathy that Smith, Pocock, and, it seemed, most of the others in the class felt for him – it rather unsettled me that they could take against anyone so strongly, purely because he didn't have the same status or, presumably, wealth as they did. I had been brought up rather to meet people on their merits; my father was one who would as easily chat with a filthy-dirty foundry worker from Lucy's at the end of his shift as with a local councillor or a captain of industry. Perhaps that was one reason why he always got such enthusiasm and loyalty from the men who worked for him.

Maybe it was partly that streak of rebelliousness in me that made me persist in trying to befriend him. But there was something about Jake, that air of stolid self-sufficiency, which appealed to me; during those classes, I covertly studied him, taking in the unruly thatch of hair which fell between light brown and gold in colour, the tanned complexion, the not-unpleasing profile with a strong chin and slightly upturned nose; and, on the rare moments when they turned to me, his startling eyes, more turquoise than blue. This was someone, I thought, that I *could* perhaps welcome as a friend, if he would unbend enough to talk to me!

When we went to board the bus that evening, I deliberately waited and followed him up the steps. He sat by a window, half-way down the aisle; as I sat beside him, he glanced up at me, the look of wary puzzlement in his face again, only to turn and gaze out of the window. It took me a while to pluck up the courage to try again to engage him in conversation; we were almost at the first village, where we lost a couple of passengers and gained the noisy chatter of the kids from the primary school, before I asked tentatively:

'Is it right, Jake, your Dad's a lock-keeper on the canal?'

He turned, and the wariness was tinged with a hint of anger: 'What if he is? He works bloody hard, and he does a damned good job!'

I recoiled, upset by his aggressive tone: 'Sorry – I don't mean to be rude!'

He gazed at me, the wariness fading, to be replaced with the hint of a smile again:

'That bastard Smith's been getting at you, hasn't he? Perhaps you should listen to him – his folk are more in your class, if your Dad's got his own business.' A tone of bitter resentment underlay his irony. I was startled by his use of swear-words, something I had been brought up to think of as unacceptable in any company; but, more than that, my own anger at Smith's attitude, and his attempted interference, rose to the surface: 'He's a jumped-up prat – I don't see why I *should* listen to him!'

This elicited a real, amused smile from Jake; he hesitated, then shook his head: 'Sorry, I just get so used to the other kids putting me down because my Dad's a boatman. They mostly come from families with plenty of money, and their fathers are people… you know?'

I sensed what he was getting at: 'People like Smith you mean, who think they're important?'

Now, he actually laughed: 'Yeah, that's right!'

We sat smiling at each other for a moment; and I knew, even then, that I had indeed found the friend I needed in my new home. I didn't care about his background, whether his family were rich or poor - far from it; his father's job aroused a curiosity in me, in fact, which had already annoyed Smith and his friend earlier.

That curiosity drove me to ask: 'So what does your Dad actually *do?*'

Jake gave me a thoughtful look: 'You don't know much about the canal, do you?'

'No, I don't, I'm afraid. I know it comes through Kidlington, near my Dad's factory – and it goes on into Oxford, doesn't it?'

'Yeah, that's right. It comes by here, too – through Banbury; and close by Burdon Leigh. My father's lock-keeper at Burdon Lock – he looks after the lock itself, keeps it tidy, and painted, and helps passing boats through a lot of the time; and nowadays, he has to keep an eye on the cut each side, and the first locks above and below, too. He cuts the grass, and trims the hedges, as well.'

'Sounds like a lot of work?'

'Yeah, keeps 'im busy, all right.'

I hesitated, not wanting to sound ignorant, but a term he'd used twice now puzzled me: 'What do you mean when you talk about the cut?'

He looked at me, amusement in his eyes, before replying: 'It's an old boater's term for the canal – canals are man-made, you know? They were cut out of the ground, and filled with water; so – the cut!'

'Oh – yeah, I see.'

He grinned at my embarrassment, but said: 'I bet your Dad's job has lots of words I wouldn't know, either?'

I echoed his grin now, pleased by his understanding: 'Yeah, I guess so!'

The bus was just pulling to a halt on Burdon Leigh green; along with the other kids who had boarded there that morning, Jake and I climbed down to the ground. I had my smart new leather satchel; he slung a scruffy canvas bag over his shoulder, gave me a grin: 'Come on then – we go the same way, don't we?' I nodded, and we set off the short distance to my new home.

'Which way do you go to get home, Jake?' I asked.

'Past your house, then down the track by Manor Farm.'

I recalled the bridleway which the girls had talked me out of exploring the previous week: 'The path that goes round behind the big barn?'

'Yeah, that's it. I go across two fields, then turn left along another footpath – that goes to the lock.'

'How far is it?'

'Oh – about a mile and a half, all told.'

'You have to walk all that way, every day?'

Jake gave me a grin, amused by the disbelief in my voice: 'Yeah – morning and evening!'

'Can't your Dad give you a lift to the bus?'

He stopped, turned to face me; there was a flash of

anger in his eyes before it faded into patient tolerance: 'Listen, Harry – He hasn't got a car, okay? We're *poor,* you understand? My Dad just about earns enough to keep us, we can't afford luxuries. We don't have a television set, or a fridge, or a washing machine – they wouldn't be much use, anyway, 'cause there's no electricity where we live. And the car wouldn't be any use either – there's no road to our house! Now, do you understand?'

I stood gaping at him, amazed that in the advanced world of the nineteen-fifties, there were still people who didn't have electricity in their homes. I know, now, that it wasn't that uncommon; but I had been brought up in the big city, and it hadn't occurred to me that others might not have the same kind of lifestyle that we did. The houses and cottages of the village had a supply; and mains gas, as well.

'I'm sorry, Jake – I didn't mean…'

He cut me off: 'I know you didn't, Harry.' He turned, and started walking again; I tagged along as he went on: 'You're the first kid who's asked about it without being nasty. But if you'd rather make friends with some of the others, I'd understand, okay?'

We were outside my house, by the garden gate. I paused to open it, then turned to look at him. All that day, the other kids who had spoken to me had all regarded me as some kind of curiosity, like lepidopterists with a rare specimen of butterfly in their nets – I suppose it went with being the new boy, but it supported my resolve as I replied:

'I wouldn't rather. All right?'

There was a tightness to his jaw as he stared at me,

gave me a sudden, sharp nod: 'All right.' He stood there a moment longer, as if unsure what to say next; then, he turned away: 'See you tomorrow.'

'Yeah – see you in the morning.' I watched him walk away, without a backward glance, past the farm, and then disappear behind the old stone-built barn.

Chapter Four

That evening, my parents were eager to know how I'd got on in my first day at the County High. Over dinner, I answered their questions about the different lessons, what my form master was like, and the other kids. I answered that one with a shrug, and a non-committal mumble; for some reason I couldn't have explained, I felt reluctant to talk about Jake. Perhaps I was aware, deep down, that his acceptance of me was fragile, that our initial tentative contact could easily be lost.

After dinner, while my mother was in the kitchen, washing the dishes, my father leant back in his chair and lit his habitual cigarette. He looked up at me from under lowered brows as he put the match to it, and said:

'You didn't like it much at St Peter's, did you, Harry?'

I shook my head: 'No, Dad, not much. Most of the other boys were so…' I trailed off, unsure of the words I needed to express my feelings.

'Snobbish?' He completed my sentence for me.

'Yeah – and all in their own little groups, all the time, making fun of everyone else, if you see what I mean?'

'Yeah. Cliquey.' I wasn't quite sure what that meant, but I nodded all the same. He repeated his earlier question, put during dessert: 'What are the kids like at your new school, then?'

I hesitated, not wanting to criticise the school they'd chosen to send me to: 'Some of them seem okay.'

'But some of them aren't?' I nodded, reluctantly.

'There're a few of the snobs there, too, are there?' My Dad always had a way of getting to what I was feeling.

'There are, yes, Dad.'

'Mm. Well, best thing to do is just ignore them, and try to make friends with the sensible ones. Right?'

'Right, Dad.'

'So – have you made friends with anyone, yet?'

I hesitated, but then admitted: 'Well, maybe, Dad.'

'Early days, yet, is it?'

I nodded, relieved that he seemed to understand: 'Yes, Dad.'

'Anyone I'd know?'

'I don't think so, Dad.'

He held my eyes, then nodded slowly, accepting my reluctance to say more: 'All right, Harry. Just remember, true friendship is the most valuable thing in the world, more important than money, or prestige, or how big your house is – understand?' It was as if he could see right through my skull, pick out what I was thinking. And his words reassured me that my friends would be acceptable to him, whoever they were; I just smiled, and nodded, and he waved me off to my usual task of drying the dishes for my mother.

* * *

It was raining, next morning, as I made my way down to the green for the school bus. I stood there, dripping quietly, with the two girls, two little boys, and the shop-keeper's teenage son, wondering where Jake was; like the day before, he hurried up just as the bus arrived, water running from his sodden hair and glistening on the old, battered macintosh which looked to be about three sizes too big for him. I led the way up the steps, and took a seat by a window; he flopped down beside me, shaking his head to dispel the rain from his hair.

He laughed as he saw me duck: 'Sorry! Didn't mean to give you a shower like that!'

I grinned at him: 'Doesn't matter – I was wet enough already!'

He looked me up and down: 'That's a nice coat.'

'Yeah.' I suddenly felt awkward, embarrassed by the smartness of my attire when he was clearly wearing some old hand-me-down: 'My old mac didn't fit, so my Mum bought me a new one in the holidays.'

'Very nice' he repeated – I couldn't hear any trace of envy, or irony, in his tone, and it suddenly occurred to me that if I wanted his friendship, I would have to work as hard as him not to let our different backgrounds get in the way. At that point, I still felt, I suppose, that I was the superior one, with my relatively-wealthy parents and comfortable lifestyle – I had yet to appreciate the wealth *he* enjoyed; or even, if I tell the truth, to have the vaguest idea of what his lifestyle was really like. I kept my own voice neutral as I replied:

'Thanks.'

He delved into the old canvas bag: 'What have we got today?' The rest of the journey into school was taken up by discussion, speculation, about the day's lessons.

It was still drizzling at break time – we all sat disconsolately in the form-room, joining in a general discussion about the double period of maths we had just enjoyed – if enjoyed was the right word! By lunchtime, the rain had eased; I went for my prepared meal, wondering what awful concoction we would be served this time, while Jake once again disappeared outside somewhere. Once fed, feeling just as full and disappointed as the day before, I found him again sitting on the concrete structure outside the door, and hopped up beside him, this time without asking.

He looked around: 'Hi, Harry. How was dinner?'

I grimaced: 'Awful!'

'Glad I don't have them, if they're that bad!'

'I wish *I* didn't – what do you have?'

'Oh, I bring my own sandwiches.' Just at that moment, a group of other first-year boys sauntered past, Smith and Pocock among them; they obviously overheard what we were saying, because Smith spoke up, making sure that I could hear:

'Of course, some of us *can't afford* school dinners, you know.'

'You have to feel sorry for them, don't you?' Pocock's voice was equally audible.

Annoyed, I raised my own voice: 'I wish I *didn't* have to have school dinners, they're so dreadful!'

Smith looked around, aping surprise at seeing me: 'Oh, Turner! Didn't see you there! Trying to find out how the poorer classes live, are you?'

'My father's always said that it's *who* you are that matters, not what you've got!' I retorted.

'Admirable, I'm sure! But be careful, sitting there, you might pick up the same smell!'

'Why don't you just bog off, and leave him alone, you snobbish swine?' I jumped off the dais onto my feet as I spoke.

Smith raised his hands in mock astonishment: 'I thought I was talking to *you,* Turner! And I was referring to the smell from the *drains,* of course – that's what's under that box you're sitting on, you know?'

I went to take a step forward, raising my fists as I did so; but I felt my arms gripped from behind, preventing me from moving despite exerting all the strength I could muster. The little crowd of sycophants surrounding Smith wandered away, laughing; I turned to Jake:

'You should have let me hit him, the horrible pig!'

He shook his head, humour twinkling in his eyes, as he released his hold on me:

'What good would that do, Harry? He's bigger than you, you'd only get hurt; and in trouble too, for starting a fight!' He looked at me appraisingly, then went on: 'How strong are you?'

'Strong enough!'

He smiled, then knelt down by one corner of the drain box, holding one hand up, the elbow resting on its top: 'Come on – arm-wrestle me!' I just stared at him; he jerked his head at the space opposite, around the corner of the box: 'Come on!'

Reluctantly, but afraid to refuse his challenge, I knelt too, put my elbow on the box, took his hand in my own. His eyes smiled into mine; then he nodded sharply. I felt him putting pressure against my hand, and responded in kind; as he put more and more effort in, so did I, until I was at the limit of my strength. Jake sensed that that was all I had; with a grin, and an ease which I would not have believed, he flattened my arm against the concrete.

'I wasn't ready!' I protested.

Smiling, he offered: 'Again, then?'

'Okay!'

But the rematch had just the same result. If anything, he beat me even more easily than the first time. I sat back on my haunches, rubbing my weary arm, and grinned at him: 'Okay, so you're stronger than I am!'

'You see the point, Harry?' I shook my head as we rose to our feet.

'Look – I could beat Smith, or any of his cronies, into a pulp, anytime I wanted to, right? But, what if I did? That's what he *wants*, to get me angry – it would mean he'd won, don't you see? Made me lose my temper and hit him. If I can keep my cool, ignore him, then *I'm* the one in control, see? He has to keep on trying, and failing, as long as I do that!'

'Yeah – I guess so…' I could see what he was getting at, but wasn't sure if he was right. Perhaps my desire to *see* Smith beaten to a pulp was affecting my view.

Jake grinned at me: 'Turn around!' Puzzled, I did as he said, and felt him grip me by the waist. He went down on his haunches, and suddenly thrust upward, lifting me bodily until I was standing on the concrete box over the school's drains, two feet higher than I had been a moment before.

'Okay, okay, point taken!' I staggered, regained my balance, and turned to look down at his grinning face: 'Goodness, you *are* strong, aren't you?'

He just shrugged: 'I have to help my Dad a lot of the time, keeps me fit, I suppose.'

I looked at him with a new respect – even as a child, I could see that someone who had the ability to defend himself so easily, but exercised such restraint in the face of constant taunts, had to be a pretty special sort of person, in more ways than one.

He was looking uncomfortable, as if embarrassed at having shown off like that; I held out a hand: 'Hey?'

He looked up and grinned, reached out and helped me down to ground level, clapping me on the back with his free hand as I grinned back at him. At that moment, the bell rang for the resumption of classes, and we turned, with a new, stronger camaraderie, to go and collect our books for the next lesson.

Chapter Five

That day after school, we piled onto the bus again with all the other kids heading home to the villages and farms on the route. Jake and I were sat in a pair of seats near the front again; with lessons over for the day, my thoughts returned again to the subject of the canal, and his father's job. I felt hesitant about broaching the subject, still afraid of touching upon his sensitivity about it, but my fascination led me to risk that:

'How did your father come to be working on the canal?'

Jake turned to look at me: 'You're really interested, aren't you?' He sounded mildly surprised, as if he'd only then realised that. He gazed at me for a moment, as if trying to decide whether to talk about it – probably remembering the attitude of the other boys, and unsure if I might not turn his words against him, as they would undoubtedly do.

But then he said: 'Okay – if you want to know, Harry: We used to have our own boats – my Dad worked for Grand Unions, back during the war, had a pair, running munitions from Birnigum to Brentford, then back-loading with all sorts of stuff – aluminium ingots, steel tube, sugar, you name it. When the gov'ment nationalised everything, he went with the Transport Commission, worked boats for them for a while; but then my Mum died, and he couldn't manage a pair any more – I was just a little kid, then. They let him run a single motor – the loads were getting fewer, anyway, by then. But then he had his accident…'

'Accident?' I queried.

'Yeah – he got caught when someone tipped a wagon full of coal into the boat, buried him, almost. They got him out; but his arm was all smashed up, beyond fixing. They cut it off, in Coventry Hospital. The comp'ny gave 'im the job here, then, 'cause he couldn't work a boat any more, not with just me to help – I was only seven, then. We've been here ever since. That's why I'm in a class with kids who are all younger than me – I didn't start school properly 'til I was eight.'

His explanation had thrown up so many questions that I didn't know where to start; or even, if I should! I was burning with curiosity about so many of the things he'd said, but I didn't want to seem to be prying. I decided that the safe thing was to ask about the less personal things, for the moment:

'What d'you mean by a pair, Jake?'

He looked at me with a slightly condescending smile: 'A pair of boats, Harry! Working boats on the cut usually run in pairs, right? One with a motor, and one without, towed behind on a line – that way, you get the most cargo moving in one go, see? Fifty tons, you can get on a pair! A single motor is just what it sounds like – a motor boat, working on its own, without a butty.'

'A butty is the one you tow along, then?'

'Yeah! You're getting the idea!'

'You still have boats working on the canal?'

'Oh yeah! Not as many as there used to be, now, but

some still come this way, mostly to Banbury, with coal for the Co-op, or to the tar works.'

The bus stopped, to off-load the first passengers and pick up the primary school kids. As it pulled away again, I asked: 'You haven't got any sisters or brothers, then?'

'Nah. Might have had, if my Mum hadn't died, of course.'

'Just you and your father?'

'Mm.'

Sensing that he seemed reluctant to expand on that point, I went back to something else I'd been wondering about: 'If you haven't got any electricity in your house, what do you do for lights at night?'

He laughed: 'Oil lamps! We haven't got gas, either.'

This astonished me further: 'What do you cook on, then?'

'The range, of course! Like we had in the boats, but this one's much bigger.' Seeing the puzzled look on my face, he went on: 'We burn coal, or wood – keeps us warm in the winter, cooks our meals all year round.'

Feeling that I'd poked my nose into his way of life enough for one day, I fell silent. I had little idea of what the canal was actually like – I'd only caught the odd glimpse of the narrow channel of still water from the roads on trips in my father's car around Kidlington or Oxford. The idea of a whole world which I knew nothing about, of boats passing up and down, carrying all kinds of unknown cargoes, in such apparent obscurity but so close to where I and many others, probably equally ignorant, all had our lives, fascinated me beyond description. I resolved to find out as much as I could from my new friend about this hidden world, over the days and weeks to come.

The bus stopped on the green; we all piled out again, and set off in our different directions, Jake and I together as far as my front door, walking in companionable silence. At the gate we parted again; this time, he looked back with a wave as he turned the corner to vanish behind the barn.

* * *

That night the atmosphere at dinner was comfortable as my mother served up the pork chops. Like many housewives of those days, she stayed at home all day, making a life out of keeping the house and the garden – she joined the village's W.I., and soon became a stalwart of that admirable organisation. She certainly had no need, with my father's income, to go out to work, as so many women do today.

Looking back now, I realise that she was a handsome woman, tall and slender, with her dark curly hair, deep brown eyes and almond-shaped face; she certainly looked the part, on the odd occasions when the two of them got dressed up to go out to some business function, in an elegant dress, her arm through my father's as he wore one of his smartly-cut grey suits. But then, to me, she was just Mum.

Over the dessert, she asked me: 'Who was the boy I saw you with this afternoon, Hal?' She was the only one who would call me Hal; I was always Harry to my father – or Henry, if I was in trouble!

I raised my eyes, surprised that we'd been seen: 'His name's Jake, Mum.'

'Does he live on one of the farms out this way, dear? I saw him go on out of the village.'

'Er – no, Mum…' I hesitated, afraid that she might take against him if she knew where he lived, what his father did, as the boys at school had done – but then, my father's words came back to me, his reassurance that friendship was more important than status: 'His Dad's the lock-keeper, on the canal.'

'Oh!' The surprise was clear in her tone; and there was an arch to her eyebrows which hinted at disapproval. My father smiled, and cut into the conversation:

'Friends, are you, Harry?'

'Yes, Dad.'

'Then that's all that matters, isn't it, Gloria?' My mother looked flustered for a moment, but then smiled at me: 'Of course it is, dear!' My Mum, God bless her, had all the makings of a snob; but my father had a way of bringing her down to earth.

He turned to me again: 'How long has he been at this lock, do you know?'

I tried counting back through the story Jake had told me earlier: 'About five years, I think. Before that, he had his own boat.'

'Hmm.' He gave me an appraising look: 'Boatman, was he? How about Jake's Mum?'

'She's dead, Dad. There's just Jake and his Dad – and *he's* only got one arm, he had an accident on the boat. That's why he's a lock-keeper now, 'cause he couldn't manage the boat any more.'

'He sounds like an interesting fellow – are you going out to meet him, sometime?'

I shrugged my shoulders: 'Dunno, Dad – maybe.' My mother smiled across the table at me:

'If Jake's your friend, Hal, you can always invite him here, whenever you want?'

'Yes, Mum – maybe I will, sometime.'

She rose, to gather the dirty plates from the table, and I got up to help as my father sat back to light his cigarette.

Chapter Six

The following morning passed uneventfully; the weather now was dry but grey and overcast. At morning break, Jake and I strolled around the perimeter of the playground, keeping out of the way of our other classmates. We didn't talk much – from the start, we seemed to have that ability to be together without having to keep a conversation going all the time – until he turned to me and said:

'I never said thank you, Harry.'

I glanced around, puzzled: 'What for?'

He smiled: 'For trying to stand up for me, yesterday!'

I shrugged: 'Oh – hey, no big deal, okay?'

He stopped, held out his hand: 'Okay. Friends, right?'

I thought we'd already established that, but I took his hand: 'Right.'

We strolled on, until the bell recalled us to lessons.

At lunch, after we'd gone our separate ways to eat, we sat again, side by side, on the raised drain-covers. I had in mind to ask more questions about his life, but he pre-empted me:

'I've told you all about me, Harry – what about you? Where did you come from?'

I told him all about the move from Oxford, the big house we'd had on the Woodstock Road; I talked about my father's engineering business, and the factory in Kidlington, about how much I'd hated going to St Peter's, about my old primary school, about the friends I'd left behind. He listened in sympathetic silence; when I ran out of words, he said:

'Burdon Leigh must seem like a real dump to you, after the city?'

'I thought it was, at first. But...' I shrugged: 'It's *different,* but it has its good points!' I went on to tell him that I had enjoyed exploring around the fields and farms – I *didn't* say that the blossoming of our friendship had been the major redeeming feature of the place. After all, that wasn't the kind of thing that boys said to each other, was it?

'You didn't come across the canal, then?'

I thought about telling him of the way the girls had put me off going down the bridleway which I now knew led to his home, but I refrained, afraid of hurting his feelings: 'I must have gone in every direction but that, I suppose!'

He nodded: 'Do you want to come and see, some time?'

I turned to him; my eagerness must have been clear in my expression as much as in my voice: 'I'd love to! Can I?'

It was his turn to shrug his shoulders: 'Sure – if you want. Saturday?'

'Yeah – you're on! Will your Dad be there?'

He raised surprised eyes to me: ''Course!'

'Great!' I think I had an image of his father, with his boating background and missing arm, as some kind of romantic pirate figure – the truth, I was to learn, was very different, if just as fascinating.

'Okay – I'll walk up and meet you, show you the way.'

'Yeah – thanks, Jake!'

With that, the bell sounded once more to summon us to our labours.

* * *

The rest of that day passed without incident; next day was Friday, and my anticipation of the visit to Jake's home was growing. But, as we arrived at school, Smith and his cronies tried a new tack:

Our bus had arrived outside the gates, and we were all debarking, trekking up the paved path to the front doors, when a voice rang out from behind us:

'There they go – the dirty boatee and the greasy engineer!'

'Make a good pair, don't they?' A second voice took up the attack; Pocock, as always following Smith's lead. Jake ignored them, carried on walking, but I turned to face them, my anger rising again, especially as the taunts were aimed at me, too, now. But as I turned, Jake's words that had followed our last near confrontation came back to me; and suddenly, the two bullies barbed comments struck me as funny. Quite why I found them so hilarious, I couldn't have said, but my angry riposte vanished in a gale of laughter. And then, of course, their incredulous expressions just made it seem all the funnier; I laughed until I could hardly stand up. Jake had turned too, now, and then he was laughing as well – we were so overcome with hilarity that we had to hold each other up. Smith and Pocock pushed past, their expressions now mirroring their disgust, which only served to set us off again; not even Smith's muttered 'we'll get the pair of you, you just wait' could dampen our humour. At last, we turned and made our way to the form room, pushing past the smiles of a number of our fellow-pupils, still chuckling and wiping the tears from our eyes.

It was that incident which put the final seal on our friendship, I think. From that moment on, I knew that we were destined to go through the rest of our schooldays as the best of friends; and, who could tell, on into adult life as well, perhaps?

The rest of that day, and so many schooldays that were to follow, were spent in each others' company, only separated in the odd classes where we had been unable to secure adjoining seats. Truth to tell, I found myself almost grateful to the clique which had gone to such trouble to put my friend down in front of the rest of our fellows, because they had, inadvertently, created that space which I could now fill.

Chapter Seven

Saturday morning saw me hanging around the cottage, getting ever more fretful. With typical schoolboy carelessness, we had neglected to set a time for our rendezvous; I'd wanted to try calling, but my father pointed out gently, before he set off for his office, that the lock cottage probably didn't have a telephone, so I just sat and waited.

It was almost ten o'clock when a tap came at the door. I rushed to open it, to find a grinning Jake on the step:

'Sorry I'm a bit late, Harry, we had an emergency this mornin', 'n I had to stop and help.' Out of school uniform, he looked surprisingly different; older, more self-confident than ever. He was wearing an old brown jacket, worn but very clean, over an almost sparkling white shirt which had no collar, and a grey flat cap, the kind which was common apparel among workmen of the day.

'Oh, that's okay.' I tried to hide the impatience I'd been feeling; my mother appeared behind me, from the kitchen where she'd been tidying up after our breakfast, and Jake's eyes rose over my shoulder.

'Mum – this is Jake, Jake Woodrow, my friend from school.'

He stepped forward, swept his cap from his head with his left hand, and held out his right: 'Mrs Turner – I'm pleased to meet you, Ma'am.'

She gave him a surprised, delighted smile, quickly wiped her own hand on her apron and took his: 'It's good to meet you, Jake. We're so glad that Hal's made a good friend here so soon – we had to leave his old friends behind in Oxford, you see?' It was an indication of her being caught off-guard for my mother to be so loquacious with someone she didn't know. She glanced at me, and I could see in her face that his chivalrous greeting had impressed her.

He gave me a quick grin: 'Oh, Harry's a good guy, Ma'am, I'm pleased you brought him here! I've asked him to come and visit my father and me, at our house, today?'

'Yes, that's fine, Jake, he's told us all about it. How long can he stop?'

'As long as he wants, Mrs Turner!'

She turned to me: 'Okay, Harry – I think you ought to get home for tea, your father will be back by then, all right?'

'Yes, Mum – about six?'

'That'll do – unless Mr Woodrow wants to get rid of you sooner! You're not to be a nuisance, you understand?'

'Yes, Mum.'

'Get along, then, and have a good time, both of you! It was nice to meet you, Jake – you must come and visit Hal here sometimes.'

'I will, Mrs Turner, if it's all right?'

'Of course, child! Any time – just make sure Hal warns me you're coming, you hear?'

'Yes, Ma'am!' She echoed his grin, an unaccustomed response for my rather straight-laced mother, and I knew that he'd made a really good impression on her. That pleased me – I had desperately wanted my friend to be acceptable with my parents, and it had been *her* reaction that had been worrying me.

We left the house, and set off to walk to the lock. Along the road, past Manor Farm, and so on to the bridleway behind the barn. As we left the road, he glanced at me, a twinkle in his eyes: *'Hal?'*

I squirmed inwardly: 'Oh, that's what my Mum calls me, sometimes. I hate it, but – She's my Mum, you know?'

'Yeah, sure.' The grin on his face was mischievous, and I knew that piece of information was going to come back to haunt me, sometime.

We walked on; neither of us spoke for a while, until I said: 'My Mum likes you.'

He looked at me, grinning again: 'That's good! She's very nice, your Mum.'

'Yeah. She can be a bit – starchy, sometimes, but she's okay, really.'

'*I* like her.' We walked on a bit further, before I asked:

'What was this emergency you had?'

'Oh, it wasn't us, exactly. Dolly, old Joe Skinner's mule, took a look on the bend a bit above our lock, and we 'ad to goo an' 'elp pull 'er out, then put 'er in the barn and give 'er a good rub-down, else she'd 'ave caught pnuemony or somethin'.'

'Sorry?' I had only followed part of this explanation; and it struck me that Jake's diction had changed, as soon as he started talking about the incident, a fact which puzzled me considerably.

He glanced at me, smiled ruefully: 'Sorry, Harry! You don't understand boater's talk, do you? Joe and Rose

Skinner work a horse-boat, with their old mule, Dolly –
she fell in, 'cause the towpath's a bit dodgy up there –
that's what we mean by 'taking a look'. And we had to get
her out, keep her warm, so she wouldn't get sick, you
understand?'

'Oh – yeah, right. She's okay, is she?'

'Yeah – they'll have gone on by now, I expect. They've
got twenty-odd ton of coal on for Banbury Co-op, and
Joe'll want to get there today, so's they can be first to
unload on Monday.'

The thought of a real cargo boat, loaded down with
coal, excited me; I was sorry to have missed seeing them:
'Will there be other boats through today?'

Jake shrugged: 'Dunno – maybe. There aren't so many,
nowadays, just Joe and Rose, a Claytons, or Willow Wren,
pair, sometimes.'

'Claytons? And Willow Wren – who are they, Jake?'

'Oh – they're two carrying companies that still run
down this way, from time to time, Willer Wrens with coal
from Coventry, for Banbury; Claytons run tar boats, to the
tar distillers there too. Joe's a number one – that mean's
he owns his own boat, you see? The *Friendship* belongs
to him and Rose, while the families who run the other
pairs only work for the companies.'

'Yeah, I see.' I thought I did; but the world of the canal
– the *cut* – was still baffling to me in so many ways. We
walked on again, while I tried to absorb, make sense of,
this fresh information, adding it to my growing store of
knowledge about the canal – I was anxious not to make
too much of a fool of myself in front of Jake's father.

We turned onto the field path from the bridleway, which

led straight on, as I was to discover later, to a bridge over the canal; now, the going was much narrower, and we had to walk in single file. As I followed Jake, I noticed more details of his clothing: His long trousers were made of a smooth-looking fabric, in a grey so dark as to be nearly black; the old jacket had neatly-stitched oval leather patches on each elbow, and a similar strip of leather around each cuff. The dark grey checked cap was pulled down tight over his unruly hair, which stuck out behind in a dark gold thatch.

I was always pretty fit, as a kid, and used to walking. But I was used to walking on smooth, surfaced streets, for the most part; it wasn't long before the tramp across the fields, on the rough, uneven surface of the bridleway, and then the narrower way of the footpath, was making my legs and ankles ache. Jake trudged on unremittingly; I noticed now that he was wearing heavy, solid-looking leather boots, much better suited to the terrain than my own light plimsolls. He realised that I was beginning to make heavy weather of it, smiled around encouragingly: 'Not far now, Harry! You okay?'

'Yeah, of course!' I made an effort to step out more confidently, and promptly tripped in an unseen depression. He helped me up, brushed the soil and leaves from my jacket and trousers, diplomatically keeping his amusement in check.

I caught his eye, and grinned ruefully: 'All right, I can't help being a townie, can I?' That set us both laughing; he clapped me on the back, told me: 'We'll soon get you trained up, Harry, don't worry!'

We set off again, and before much longer, to my relief

if I tell the truth, the lock came into sight, at the end of a track which sloped down alongside a hedgerow. I could see the square, red-brick cottage, one or two smaller brick-built outbuildings, what looked like a neat garden; and, half-hidden behind all that, the painted upper structure of the lock-gates, smart in their dramatic black-and-white against the soft greens of the spring countryside.

And at last we were there, standing at the gate from the field into what was, indeed, a neat, well-tended garden, given mostly over to vegetables although a few spring flowers bloomed along the low wall which separated the garden from the grassed lockside.

Jake called out: 'Dad! Where are you?'

'In the big barn, boy!' A voice echoed from the larger of the two outbuildings; Jake beckoned me, and led the way across to it, pushed the rickety door open. The dingy interior was stacked with all kinds of equipment, some of it familiar, but much of it strange to my townie, land-lubber eyes – and all of it looking old, battered and well-worn. A short, stocky figure was bending over a rack of odd-looking implements, which might have been garden rakes with varying lengths of handle except that the tines were so long as to be more like those of a pitch-fork. He selected one, straightened up, hefting it in his one hand, and turned to us:

'Glad ye're back, Jake – there's summat stook oonder the insoide bottom gate. Oi was gooin' ter 'ave a rake around meself, but now ye're 'ere…'

'Give us the keb 'ere, Dad, Oi'll get it! Dad – this is 'Arry, he's coom to visit today, remember?'

'Course Oi remember, d'yer think Oi'm goin' senoile

or summat? 'Ow d'yer do, 'Arry, good to see yer!' The figure stepped forward into the light, held out a square, calloused hand; I took it, felt the man's strength in his handshake, trying not to look too obviously at the other, empty sleeve of his overall, which was tucked into a pocket to stop it flapping about.

'It's a pleasure to meet you, Mr Woodrow.' He smiled at me, showing uneven, stained teeth; but the look in his eyes, the same bright turquoise blue as Jake's, was one of uncritical, open friendliness. A spotlessly-clean shirt showed through the open front of his overall, and he had a flat cap, older and more battered-looking than his son's, crammed down over his thick, dark hair. Hearing his speech, I understood the sudden change in Jake's manner of talking; his accent had a rolling, almost musical sound, not unlike the usual Oxford City dialect which has a hint of the West Country in it, but with the very soft vowels of the Midlands somehow inserted. I was to come to know this as the common sound of the boaters, in the months that followed.

And Jake's sudden switching from his school speech to this boater's dialect brought to mind one of my father's secretaries, a Glaswegian girl who always spoke with an accent as thick as marmalade, but became totally incomprehensible after even the briefest of return visits to her family. So, I now realised, did Jake slip back into his ancestral accent in his father's presence; or, it seemed, when talking about what he would call 'the cut', and its people.

'Goo give Jake a 'and wi' the keb, boy – Oi'll put the kettle on the stove. Coopa tea suit you, will it?'

'Yes, please, Mr Woodrow.'

'Goo along, then, it'll be ready when yeh coom in.'

I turned and followed Jake out onto the lockside; I found him using the odd-shaped rake – a keb, they'd called it – to drag along below the partly-open bottom gate, one side of the lock, where it would normally seat when it was closed.

He looked up as I approached: 'Things get caught under the gates, sometimes, Harry – stones, bits of tree branch, all sorts of stuff – and it stops the gates closing properly. We have to get it out, or the boats can't get through – you can't fill the lock, if the bottom gates won't shut, you see?'

'Yeah, I think so.'

'I think I've got it clear – felt like some gravel'd got swept under the cill. Push that gate shut, will you?' He indicated the balance beam nearest to me; I leant against it, felt it move slowly, ponderously, under my weight, swinging around until the gate itself stopped with a solid bump against its fellow.

'Yeah! That's got the booger! Did moy Dad mention tea?'

'He did!' I smiled at my friend's sudden relapse into his boater's accent.

'Coom on, then, let's goo an' get it!'

Chapter Eight

I trailed along behind Jake as he returned the keb to its place in the 'big barn', feeling rather bemused. His father hadn't fitted the image I'd had of him, but his instant, open acceptance of me, his cheerful expectation that I would 'goo 'n 'elp' had taken me by surprise.

Jake put the keb back in the rack, turned to me with a grin:

'Coom on, let's get that tea – Oi'm ready for a coopa!' We hurried across, round the edge of the garden and pushed into the cottage kitchen. As he waved me to a seat at the table, I looked around, amazed. I suppose I had been expecting their home to look a bit different from mine, but what I saw there felt like a whole new world: Our kitchen was brand-new, in the current style, all tiles and white enamel and chrome, shining and spotless; the kitchen in the lock cottage was just as spotlessly clean, but the only appliance was the big, gleaming black range against one of the bright, white-washed walls. Against one outside wall was an old-fashioned stone sink, with a scrubbed wooden draining-board and a single tap above it; facing it, a tall dresser, double-fronted with cupboards and drawers, the upper racks filled with decorated, ornamental plates. In the middle of the room, where we sat, was a heavy old oak table, with a plain, solid chair at each side.

Jake's father looked around from the range, where he was pouring boiling water into a big, dark brown teapot:

'Si' down, 'Arry, tea'll be 'long soon as the pot's 'ad time ter brew!' He swept up three enamel mugs from the dresser in his one hand, and plonked them unceremoniously on the table, then delved into a cupboard for the sugar-bowl: 'Milk, Jake?'

'Yes, Dad!' My friend got up and stepped through a door at the side of the kitchen, returning from the pantry with a jug in his hand. Mr Woodrow brought the teapot over, set it down, and joined us at the table, treating me to another beaming smile:

'Moved out 'ere from h'Oxford then, 'Arry?'

'Yes, Mr Woodrow.'

'Settlin' in okay, are you?'

'Yes, sir.' He raised his eyebrows, with an amused glance at his son:

'Sir, eh? Noo need to be so formal, boy, you're not in school now! 'Ow are you liking it, in the country, then?'

'I'm *getting* to like it, Mr Woodrow.'

He caught the look which passed between me and Jake, gave a great bellow of laughter: 'Good fer you, boy! You'd not coom across the cut before, then?'

I shook my head: 'Not really; I mean, I didn't *know* anything about it, before.'

He nodded, regarded me levelly for a moment: 'It's a different world 'ere, boy – *our* world…' he looked across at his son, back at me: '*Soom* folks 'ere moight not welcome you, not a kid off the bank – But *Oi'm* glad teh see yeh. Jake 'asn't got many friends, it'll do 'im good to 'ave someone 'is own age around a bit. Ye're welcome 'ere, as offen as yeh want to coom, all roight?'

'Yes – thank you!'

He gave me a toothy grin, reached out and began to pour the tea: ''Elp yourself to sugar, boy. Pour the milk, then, Jake!'

I sipped at my mug of hot, sweet tea. It was stronger than I usually liked it; and I'd never drunk tea from a mug before, my mother always served our tea up at home in small, decorative cups and saucers. I was beginning to realise just how different Jake's way of life was from my own, even in such small, insignificant ways.

And the implied warning in his father's words troubled me as well as puzzling me – which folk? And why would they not like a 'kid off the bank'? It didn't seem like the time to ask – perhaps I'd find out, later – but something else he'd said reminded me of Jake's words a day or two before:

I looked up at my friend: 'You said something the other day, about being in a class with kids younger than you?' He glanced at his father; it was Mr Woodrow who replied to me:

'That's roight, 'Arry. Yeh see, when we 'ad the boat, we never stayed anywhere long enough fer 'im teh goo teh school proper-loike. Boot, after this' he nodded towards his empty sleeve 'the comp'ny gi' me the job 'ere. The good thing 'bout that was that young Jacob 'ere could get some proper schoolin'. But 'e was already noigh on eight year old boy then, see?'

'Yes, I see…'

'Well, 'e's caught oop real well, 'aven't yeh, boy?' Jake

gave me a grin, nodding a bit self-consciously, as his father went on: 'Oi'd managed to teach 'im the basics of readin' n' writin, 'cause moy ol' Ma 'ad taught *me,* yeh see – she'd married moy Dad off the bank, 'ad a good schooling in 'er day. Even so, 'e failed the 'leven-plus fust toime 'e took it; boot they let 'im 'ave another goo, the nex' year – 'n this toime, 'e sailed through, noo trouble at all! Got 'is place at County 'Igh, din't yer, boy?'

'Yes, Dad.' Jake was looking more and more uncomfortable with his father's continuing tale; Mr Woodrow turned to me again:

''Ow old are you, 'Arry?'

'Eleven – my birthday's in June.'

'There ye go, then! Jake's twelve, 'e'll be thirteen in September, so 'e's near a year older than you, and all the other kids in 'is class. Boot 'e was *two* year be'ind when 'e started, see? It's all down to 'is late start with 'is schoolin'.'

'Oh, right.' I looked across at Jake: 'And I thought it was just because he was stupid!' My friend's jaw dropped, and a stunned look came into his eyes; I regretted my words the moment they were out, could have bitten my tongue off in remorse, aware that I could have just lost myself the only friend I had in Burdon Leigh. The facetious comment had been automatic, a reflection, perhaps, of just how much at home I felt with the two of them – that kind of mutual joshing, verging on real rudeness, had been an integral part of my little circle of friends back in Oxford, had been a mainstay of my relationship with my best mate, Nicky, especially. But here, and now...?

The silence held for an eternal moment; but then, Jake

looked around at his father, and his face cracked into a huge grin. Mr Woodrow caught my eye, threw his head back and burst into peals of laughter:

'You'll do, boy, you'll do!' Jake was laughing, too, now; I joined in, heartily relieved, as he threatened, chuckling: 'You wait, Turner, you just wait!'

Mr Woodrow drained his mug of tea, banged the empty down on the table: 'Coom on, you two! Finish yer tea; Oi got a rackety paddle on Slat Mill wants changin', and grass wants cuttin', so we've plenty to be at!'

Jake and I finished our drinks, and got up to follow him out of the house: 'Slat Mill's the next lock up' Jake explained 'and Dad looks after that one as well, along with Bourton, the next one down.'

We met his father emerging from the bigger of the two barns, a heavy iron rack with a double row of cast-in teeth down one side in his hand, a tool-bag slung over his shoulder, and trudged off happily behind him, northwards along the towpath for the half-mile walk to Slat Mill Lock.

* * *

The rest of that day passed so quickly that it seemed as though someone had stolen a large part of it while I wasn't looking. All too soon, I looked at my wrist-watch and saw that I would need to hurry if I was not to be late home – and I didn't want to upset my mother, I wanted her to let me come out to Burdon Lock, to visit my new friend and his strange but wonderful father, as often as possible. We'd spent our day working, helping him fit that new rack to the worn paddle-gear at the other lock, taking turns with the aged, push-along lawnmower, weeding in the flower-beds and vegetable patch around his cottage – but it hadn't seemed like work at all, with Jake's company, and his father's continual, encouraging banter. I still hadn't seen a boat travelling on the canal, but even so, I couldn't wait to go there again – maybe next time, I would!

Jake insisted on walking all the way home with me, to make sure, he said, that I didn't get lost. I didn't argue too strongly; I was pleased to be able to have his company for that extra half hour. He left me at the garden gate, refusing my urging to come in and have a drink, at least, and got me a gentle telling-off from my mother for not insisting.

Chapter Nine

During the following week, my life began to settle into a routine. After the upheaval of moving house, and the excitement of starting at my new school, things took on a steadier, easier note.

At school, I was becoming just one of the crowd, accepted by my fellows after their initial curiosity had been satisfied; even Smith and Pocock were leaving me and Jake alone. I didn't suppose that they had forgiven us for the incident on the school steps, for the embarrassment our laughter had caused them; but, at the same time, I think that event had given them pause for thought, made them wary of us. I didn't care, just as long as they left the two of us in peace to enjoy our friendship.

In school, of course, Jake and I were now inseparable; the only exception being at lunch, when he would sit outside to eat his sandwiches, while I joined the rest of my classmates in the refectory. Our hunger dealt with, we would then invariably assume our private perch on top of the drain covers, to talk or sit in companionable silence, as the mood took us.

Thursday evening, he stopped for tea. On the Sunday, over our family tea-table, my mother had suggested that he might like to stop for a quick sandwich and a drink, on his way home from school – she always had something ready for me then, as we didn't have our dinner until later, after my father got in from work. A snack to keep me going, she called it; an excuse for her to stop for a cup of tea, was my unexpressed view. Be that as it may, she wanted Jake to join us, so I duly passed the invitation on, on Monday morning. It took me until Thursday to persuade him to accept; he was very reluctant to, as he saw it, take advantage – I was to realise before very long that his father was the same, not one to take anything unless he could see a way of repaying, of balancing the books, at least in his own mind.

My mother served us up tea and cheese sandwiches, and looked quite put out when I started to snigger. Jake, ever diplomatic, kept a straight face; but I caught the look in his eye – my mother's thin, delicate sandwiches and light china cups were a strange contrast with the doorstep cheddar and crusty bread, and mugs of tea that his father had treated us to during my Saturday visit.

As we munched and sipped, she said: 'Would you like to stop longer, have some dinner with us one evening, Jake?'

He put down his cup and smiled at her: 'I'd love to, Mrs Turner, but I usually have some things to do for my father when I get home. He's only got one arm you see, and there are some things he needs me to help him with.'

'I know, Jake – but surely he could spare you for an odd evening, every now and then?'

'I'm not sure, Mrs Turner – I'll ask him. It's very kind of you to offer.'

'Not at all! The way Hal went on about his visit to you last Saturday, I imagine you'll be having to put up with him at your house as often as your father will allow it!'

'I hope so – I don't have many friends who want to come and visit!'

Our quick meal over, he got up to go, apologising to my mother for having to rush away. At the gate, I reminded him to ask about stopping for dinner one night; he gave me a withering look: 'I've *said* I'll ask my Dad, Harry. It's up to him – but I expect he'll say yes, even if it has to wait for a day when he can spare me. All right?'

'Yeah, okay. I hope it's soon – I'd love you to meet *my* father!'

'Yeah, me too. You're coming over, Saturday?'

'Can I?'

''Course. Can you find your own way without a guide, do you think? Only, I usually tidy up at home while Dad gets started outside.'

''Course I can!'

He grinned, pleased to have riled me after my jibe at him in front of his father: 'We'll see you there, then – 'bout nine?'

'Sure! But aren't you coming to school tomorrow?'

'Yeah – I'll see you there, as well. But it's a date, for Saturday, right?'

'Right!'

* * *

And that Saturday, I achieved my ambition to see a boat pass through. We were up at Slat Mill Lock again, this time helping Mr Woodrow repaint the gates, when Jake glanced up, then reached over and prodded me: 'Look!'

In the distance, coming from the direction of Burdon Lock and Banbury, was the towering prow of a narrowboat. I could see a figure at the helm, and what looked like another boat, tight up behind the first; a steady tug-tug-tug-tug-tug sound carried across the water to our ears.

Jake's father looked up: 'Tha'll be Shoines, on their way back oop.'

'When'd they goo down, Dad?'

'Two days back – whoile you was suppin' tea wi'the gentry!' He feigned surprise as his son waved a threatening paintbrush at him, both grinning like Cheshire cats in my direction.

As the boats drew closer, Jake and I pushed open the bottom gates; a wave of thanks from the man at the tiller, and the front boat slid quickly in as he cast off the lines securing the second to its stern. Water boiled underneath as he brought it to a stop, the high stem against the cill below the top gate; we heaved the gates closed again as the boatman stepped up from the cabin roof onto the lockside and strode to the top paddles. He wound one up, as Jake's father raised the other; the boat held its station, the engine still ticking over in forward gear, and the boatman turned to us:

''Ow're you, young Jake? 'Oo's yer friend, then?'

Jake gave him a beaming grin: 'Oi'm foine, Frank – 'Ow're you 'n Betty? Rachel wi' yeh?'

'She's in butty cabin, gettin' tea brewed! Y'avin' one wi' us?' Jake glanced at his father, who nodded, smiling widely at this repartee.

'Can moy mate coom along?'

''F'e's a mate o' yours, course 'e can! What's yer

name, boy?' The boatman addressed me directly.

'Harry, sir.'

The man burst out laughing: 'There's noo sirs on the cut, boy! Oi'm Frank Shoine, n' that's Betty, moy missus, back there on the butty. Ye'll meet our Rachel in a whoile.'

The lock was full, the boat, still driving forwards, gently edging the top gate open. Frank Shine and Mr Woodrow closed the paddles, and the boatman stepped onto the stern, bringing the boat to a stand just clear of the lock. As Mr Woodrow leant his back against the gate's balance beam, pushing it closed, a short and very round woman in a pinafore and enormous skirt energetically wound up first one and then the other bottom paddle, the ornate bonnet on her head bobbing up and down as she did so.

'Coom on, 'Arry!' Jake beckoned me to follow him; we ran down to the second boat, where he grabbed the rope attached to a t-stud from the tiny front deck and wound it over his shoulders, his arms at full stretch. I stepped in behind him, followed his example, guessing what was afoot; between us, we pulled the empty boat forward and into the lock, climbing the steps by the gates as it slid along below us. The boatwoman took a heavy line from the stern, and braked the boat to a halt by winding it around a massive wooden bollard beside the gate. Moments later, the top paddles were up again, water flooding into the lock, the boat rising quickly.

The woman turned to us: 'Thanks, Jake – 'oo's yer mate?'

'This is 'Arry, Bet. 'E's moy mate from school.'

'School, eh? Coomin' on fer a cuppa, are yeh?'

'Please, Bet! Dad's said as it's okay.'

''Op on, then; Rachel'll 'ave it brewin' boy now.'

Jake stepped over the high gunwale into a small well behind the boat's cabin; I followed him. A girl of about sixteen looked out, smiled, and beckoned us to go in; we sat on a narrow bench at the right, crammed close together, as Jake made the introductions.

By now, the butty was clear of the lock; Frank Shine on the motor boat quickly picked up the tow again, his wife stepped into the rear of the butty, and we were on our way. Over mugs of strong sweet tea, I learnt that Rachel was their youngest daughter, the only one still working the boats with them; that they worked for a company called Willow Wren, a name I remembered Jake mentioning before; that they'd unloaded coal at Banbury Co-op the day before, and were now on their way back, unloaded, to Coventry, to wait for instructions to load again at one of the Warwickshire collieries.

Both Betty Shine and her daughter were cheerful, jolly people, the girl pretty in her own, rather weatherbeaten way, but unquestionably destined to be as round as her mother in later life. Their cabin was spotlessly clean – the tiny range, a miniature version of the one in Mr Woodrow's kitchen, glistened blackly in one corner, and brass and pretty hanging plates glittered all around. We eagerly downed our tea – both of us had been ready for a break, and a drink – and then Jake stood up, saying we'd better be getting back. We stepped out into the well again; a bridge was just approaching, and Betty used the massive wooden tiller to swing the stern of the boat in close to the towpath so that we could step off.

'Goo steady, Jake – we'll see yer agen, Oi 'ope, 'Arry?'

'I hope so too, Mrs Shine!' She gave us a cheery wave as the boats swept away, around a gentle curve in the canal. I stood and watched them go, enthralled by my first experience of the working boats and their people, until Jake gave me an unceremonious prod in the ribs: 'Coom on, we've a bit of a walk!'

We hiked back to the lock, talking non-stop, Jake explaining more about the boats and how they were worked, and about some of the other boat-people he knew, in response to my eager questions. His father greeted us with a cheerful 'back agen, then?' and handed our paintbrushes to us.

Chapter Ten

It took a couple of weeks, and some extra prompting from me, before Jake took up that invitation to dinner. And when it happened, I was left with a feeling of unmitigated disaster.

Jake had stopped in for a cup of tea and a sandwich before heading on to his home several times, but, that day, I felt that he was less than comfortable. After our quick snack, I got to show him over the house and gardens; as we passed from room to room, and then out into my mother's beautifully-tended garden, I could sense his feeling of dislocation growing. I suppose, while I was by now well aware of the differences in our lifestyles, I hadn't given a thought to how it would seem from his side of the divide; now, I began to realise how strange and even exotic our way of life would look to him, with all the comforts and conveniences we took for granted. I began to feel awkward myself, and tried even harder to make him feel at home - probably only serving to make matters worse.

Even the garden – by the time we stepped out into the bright evening, to be greeted by my mother's riot of spring flowers, I was hoping this would ease his discomfort. But, in contrast to the lockhouse garden, we had not a vegetable in sight, which must have only emphasised our relative wealth, that we could afford to buy all our food and didn't have to grow what we could, in order to make ends meet.

We retired to my room, and played a board game until my father came home. He greeted Jake warmly enough, but I felt a kind of reserve in him, which I had not expected; Jake was his usual polite self, of course. Things didn't improve over dinner, either. I've already said that my mother liked the trappings of polite society – she had prepared an excellent meal for us, with soup to start and lamb chops to follow. Jake was clearly fazed by the array of serving dishes full of vegetables, and hesitant to help himself even when encouraged to do so; and the selection of sparkling cutlery put him in a state of embarrassment, only eased when I nudged him with my elbow and gestured surreptitiously for him to follow my lead.

We reached the end of the meal, without any actual, obvious disasters; but, while he had made all the correct noises along the way, I knew that Jake hadn't really enjoyed it. About eight o'clock, when we were relaxing with a cup of coffee, he said that he ought to be getting back, to make sure his father was all right. My father shook his hand again; my mother told him he must come for dinner again another day. I saw him out to the front gate, knowing in my heart that the evening hadn't gone well, afraid that he might be put off our friendship; as we said goodnight, promised to meet on the school bus the next morning, he seemed unusually subdued, making me feel even worse.

And back indoors, things went from bad to worse. My father waved me to sit down at the table again; my mother fussed around, clearing the table, saying that it was a shame

Jake had had to go so soon, he would have been welcome to stay with me for a bit longer, perhaps he would another time… She disappeared into the kitchen; my father, his habitual cigarette in his hand, looked over at me:

'You're very fond of Jake, aren't you, Harry?'

Fond might not have been the word I would have chosen, but the gist of it was right: 'Yes, Dad.'

'Hmm. Listen, son – I don't want to upset you, but… Jake's people are, what we call itinerant. They're used to moving around, moving *on,* all the time, do you see?' I shook my head, wondering if he was trying to say that he didn't like my friend; he went on: 'I'm sure he likes you as much as you like him, Harry – but, I don't want you to be hurt and upset if his friendship wanes, if he goes on to someone else, you understand?'

'*No,* Dad! He might have moved around a lot, when they had their boat, but they don't any more! They live in the house by the lock, now, all the time, they're not going to move! He's my friend – we're *always* going to be friends!' I jumped to my feet – he reached out to me, but I dodged away, ran up to my room, feeling as if my world was falling apart, almost in tears. I knew that he didn't understand, hadn't seen the way the other kids all avoided my friend, leaving him with no other companions he might turn to, but still his apparent rejection of Jake hurt me deeply. And, given my father's normal views on equality, it had come out of the blue…

A few minutes later, the door opened quietly, and my mother came in. She sat on the edge of my bed, where I was lying staring at the ceiling, put her gentle hand on my brow: 'Harry? Dad didn't mean to upset you, he's just worried about you. Your happiness means so much to us, you know?'

I raised myself on one elbow: 'Then why did he say he doesn't like my friend?'

'He didn't *say* that, Hal! He didn't mean it, either – all he meant was… He's concerned that you're putting too much store by his friendship, that you ought maybe to look for more than one friend here, that's all, you see?'

'No, Mum! I don't want any other friends, I don't *need* them, not with Jake!' I lay back down, turned my head away; she stroked my hair for a moment, then got up, bent to kiss my forehead, and left me alone.

I went down for supper, my usual biscuit and tea, about nine – I was expected to be in bed by then, as a rule, but no-one had chased me that night, perhaps aware of my fragile mood. I don't think I spoke, other than to thank my mother for the tea – I was still angry at my father, and went to bed feeling little better. I tossed and turned; heard them make their own way to their room, and, once I thought they would be settled, got out of bed to answer an urgent need for the toilet.

Tiptoeing past my parents' room, I heard them in conversation; the tones were not exactly angry, but my mother was clearly having a go at my father:

'You didn't need to go upsetting Hal like that, Teddy!'

I heard his sigh: 'I know, Gloria, I didn't mean to! I'm just afraid that boy will turn out to be a fickle friend, you must understand?'

'I *don't*, Ted! I *like* him, he's a really nice kid, whatever his background.'

'He *is;* but… his kind of people are… unreliable. They're not used to stable relationships, you must see that? It's in their nature, to continually move on, meeting new people, making new friends – I don't want Harry getting hurt if that happens.'

'You're *wrong,* Teddy! I've seen more of Jake than you have, and I'm telling you he's a *good* boy, polite, well brought up, although goodness knows how his father's managed it! Look at him tonight – he was clearly uncomfortable at the table, but he didn't disgrace himself in the slightest, did he?'

'All right, but…'

'Why couldn't you have just kept quiet, let things develop as they will? Hal *will* make other friends, in time; for now, let him enjoy Jake's company without putting the mockers on it, can you? He loves his Saturdays out on the canal – and that's good for him! All that fresh air and exercise!'

My father sighed again: 'All right, Gloria. I'm sorry I said what I did, but it's said now. Now, can we change the subject?' There was a pause, and I could imagine my mother bending to kiss him, as she always did if they'd had any kind of exchange of words.

I had my wee, then tiptoed back to my room. I was pleased, relieved, by mother's defence of my friend, but still upset at my father's reluctance to accept him. I'd expected their reactions to be the other way round, my father the one to take anyone at their face value, my mother to look to their breeding or circumstances – to have him express such doubts about the only friend I had in the village had hurt me, and continued to do so, although I soon put it to the back of my mind, over the ensuing days and weeks.

The next morning, on the bus, Jake and I sat in a rather awkward silence at first; but then, we both started to talk at once.

I tried to apologise, but he quickly cut me off: 'No, Harry – it's not your fault. I'm sorry if it didn't go very well, but it's me, not you; I'm not used to… being in a house like yours, it's just so – different, you know? I just felt out of place, and… I'm sorry if I upset your Mum, she's really nice. But – I don't think your Dad likes me, does he?'

'It's not that, Jake – he's like that, with people he doesn't know, sometimes!' I made a spur-of-the-moment excuse.

'Yeah, okay. Anyway – you're coming over again tomorrow, aren't you? Dad says you're to stop for a meal with us, tomorrow night, as long as it's okay with your parents?'

I heard the hesitancy in his voice, and knew that he'd been feeling the same doubts as I had after the previous evening; I was pleased to put his mind at rest: 'Of course I am! And I'll stop – I'll square it with them, somehow.'

The grin spread across his face; I felt my own reflecting it. He nodded, gave me a playful punch in the ribs; I responded in kind, and we were treated to an admonishing glance from the bus-driver. But I was relieved, delighted, that our friendship was back on track.

Chapter Eleven

Saturday dawned grey and drizzly, but I don't recall that it dampened my eagerness one whit as I trudged across the fields to the lock cottage. Jake's father had his usual little list of tasks for us; but, since my weekend visits were becoming something of an institution, he had begun to temper his requirements so as to allow the two of us some free time to share. Not that I was too concerned – the whole world of the canal was so fascinating to me that I would cheerfully have spent all my time at whatever jobs he might have set us.

That Saturday, we helped Ernie Woodrow clear out his 'little barn', spreading its contents out across the grass while he sorted through them, selecting some items for the scrap bin, putting aside others that he felt he could usefully refurbish, all the while giving us a running commentary on where any particular piece of junk had come from and how he had come to acquire it, explaining to me as he went what each was used for, although I was already beginning to pick up a lot of snippets of knowledge about the cut and its furniture.

By lunchtime, we were pretty well finished. Lunch, as always, consisted of a big slab of crusty bread and a chunk of powerful cheddar cheese – the kind which growls at you when you unwrap it – and one of his trademark mugs of strong, sweet tea. The drizzle had stopped, and now the clouds were beginning to break; after lunch, released from our task, Jake and I wandered out onto the lockside, idly discussing what to do for the afternoon:

'Come on, Harry, let's go across to the railway for a change!'

'Are we allowed?' He gave me a scathing look:

''Course we are!' I shrugged:

'Okay – let's go, then!'

As the son of an engineer, the railway had always held my interest – from the lockside, I'd often paused to watch the trains pass on the main line, which ran no more than a field's width away. Now, I followed as Jake led the way along the towpath towards the next bridge, some way above the lock, where the bridleway from Burdon Leigh crossed the cut on its way to the level crossing and on to the distant village of Great Bourton. As we reached the bridge, he gave me a playful shove, then ran off over the top and away across the field:

'Slowcoach! Can't catch me!' I took off in hot pursuit:

'Watch me!' On our games days at school, running was the one sport at which I could at least hold my own with him. Over a short distance, my longer legs gave me the edge, even if his greater endurance would win out over half a mile or more. But here, he knew the ground, leaping and bounding across the uneven track – I had to keep my eyes glued to the path in front of me, and even then found myself losing out as I stumbled along as quickly as I could. I caught up with him by the level crossing, and flung myself on him, both of us laughing as we wrestled beside the tracks. A loud whistle and an approaching clatter made us desist and look around; a local train, headed by a little saddle-tank locomotive, was trundling towards us. As it passed, the engine driver looked out and waved:

'You lads be careful there!' He bellowed down; but the grin on his face was echoed by our own as we waved back. We sat together, panting, on the top rail of the low fence which lined the track:

'That wasn't fair!' I complained: 'You know the pathways 'round here, and I don't!' Jake laughed:

'Yeah – but I've got to beat you somehow! *I'm* supposed to be the one who's good at sports!'

'We'll have a race on the towpath, on the way back, it's flat there – I'll show you who's fastest!' His grin suddenly vanished:

'No, Harry! You *never* run on the cutside, it's too risky – you could slip, and go in, maybe bang your head and drown yourself.'

'You're just afraid of losing!' He shook his head:

'No! You ask my Dad, later. You can beat me in the hundred yards at school, okay?' I looked at him, puzzled by his vehemence – but it was an admonishment I was to remember in the months to come.

We sat and watched the trains for a while, waving to the local drivers, thrilling to the hurtling roar of the occasional express, chuckling at the interminable clatter of the goods trains, talking, in between, about things of significance only to schoolboys. At last, I checked my watch:

'Hey, it's nearly five, we'd better get back, hadn't we?'

'Yeah! Dad'll be wanting me to put the things out for dinner – come on!'

This time, we just jogged side by side along the bridleway and over the bridge, slowing to a walk on the towpath. Ernie Woodrow greeted us as we got back to the cottage:

'Joost in toime, boys! Get the knoives 'n forks, Jake – you sit yerself down, 'Arry, dinner's 'bout ready.'

He bent to the oven of the gleaming black range; I watched him, fascinated as always at the way he could manoeuvre even heavy objects with his one hand. Soon, a plateful of steaming stew landed in front of me: 'Get stook in, boy! We'll join yeh in a jiffy!'

I was as hungry as a horse; but something gave me pause – the stew looked, and smelled, absolutely fine, but I was taken aback at the sight of what appeared to be a huge potato. I should explain – given my mother's preoccupation with the finer details of life, you might expect that potatoes, in our house, came in three guises: Boiled, mashed, or possibly roasted, with the Sunday joint. Nowadays, it probably seems incredible that, at the age of eleven, I had never before met a jacket potato.

Jake, plate in hand, took his place opposite me. He looked across, puzzled at my hesitancy; following the direction of my gaze, he chuckled, putting two and two together from his own knowledge of my mother. I looked up; he gave me a grin, and indicated his own plate with a quick nod of his head. I smiled cautiously back, and followed his lead as he carved his own potato in half and smothered each exposed side in butter from the dish. His father joined us:

'That all roight for yeh, boy?' he asked me; I nodded:

'Fine, thank you, Mr Woodrow.'

'Rabbit stew – veggies out 'a the garden, and two fresh coneys! Suey Beechey dropped 'em off fer us this mornin'; Alby trapped 'em las' noight, got more'n they could use.'

'How's your potato, Hal?' Jake asked innocently. I threw him an aggrieved glance:

'Very nice, thank you!' He laughed:

'Harry hasn't had a jacket spud before, Dad' he explained.

'You *'aven't?* Blow me! Don't know what you been missin', lad!' I smiled at him:

'I know! My Mum only does them boiled or mashed – but this is much nicer!'

'You could explain, ask her to do them this way for you, Hal?' Jake's tone was all innocence, but there was an evil twinkle in his eye. His father, catching the underlying spark in his question, glanced at him, then turned his smile on me:

'Hal?'

'It's a stupid name my Mum calls me, Mr Woodrow.'

'Aaah!' He turned to his son: 'Don't you goo teasin' 'Arry, now, Jake! 'E moight get fed oop 'n not coom 'ere agen!'

'Noo fear o' that, Dad! No-one else'll 'ave 'im!'

'You can talk!' I retorted. Jake flicked a pea at me from the side of his plate, caught me over my left eyebrow: 'Greasy Engineer!'

I flicked one back, hit him on the cheek: 'Dirty Boatee!'

Ernie Woodrow was gazing from one to the other of us, as if half-afraid our insults were meant seriously; but then he saw our expressions, and burst out laughing.

He raised his hand to quell the riot:

'Settle down, the pair o' yeh! Get on wi' yer dinners n' stop boogerin' about!'

'Roight, Dad!' 'Yes, Mr Woodrow.' We subsided, grinning like idiots.

We all cleared our plates; even I succumbed to seconds of the stew, and another small potato. After a mug of tea, I gave a hand with the washing-up before deciding that I should head for home; Ernie waved me away from the depths of his armchair, through in the sitting-room of the cottage, while Jake came out to see me off:

'See you Monday, then?'

'Yeah – thanks for today, the dinner was super.' He grinned:

'Hey, it'll be half term in a few weeks, won't it?'

'Er, yeah… Two weeks time, I think. Why?'

'Well – why don't you come and stay? For a day or two, at least?'

'What – stay *here? Sleep* here?'

'Of course, if it's too rough and… and *uncivilised* for you…'

'No, 'course not! It'd be *brilliant!*'

'There's a spare bed in my room – it's probably not as comfortable as yours, mind…'

'I don't care! I'm sure Mum won't mind – it'll be *excellent!*'

'I'll tell Dad, then, shall I?'

'Yeah – he won't mind, will he?'

'Nah! He'll love it – he likes you, you know.'

As I made my way home along the footpath, I felt that life couldn't have got any better.

Chapter Twelve

It was now early May. Half term, in those days, fell on the Whitsun weekend – today's Mayday and late Spring holidays were far in the future. But, before we could get to our mid-term break, we had to get through two more weeks of school; weeks which were to prove eventful…

* * *

It was the Tuesday following my Saturday dinner at the lock cottage, that Smith and Pocock set about making good their threats from earlier in the term. Emerging into the playground after lunch, I found Jake was unaccountably missing from his habitual perch; as I looked around for him, I heard a menacing voice behind me:

'He's not here, Turner. I heard he's been called to the office.' I turned to face Smith:

'Oh? Why, do you know?' Pocock was at his elbow, as always; two other boys, Goffin and Stokes, were with them as well. The foursome were known as the class toughs, a reputation they had set out to achieve. *Oh shit, I'm in trouble…*

'It's not a good idea to *laugh* at us, Turner. We need to make sure you remember that…'

All four of them piled in. I don't suppose it can have

lasted more than a minute, two at the most – not long enough for anyone to summon a master, anyway. But at the end, with eight fists and at least four knees in constant use, I felt as though I'd been run over by a steamroller. A crowd had quickly begun to gather, but no-one tried to step in; my four assailants scattered, leaving me leaning, breathless and bowed, against the stone wall by the door.

Sore, aching and furious, I tried to straighten up, glaring around at those who had failed to help me. Then an arm slid around my waist, a worried face looked into mine:

'Harry – what happened?' I drew a breath, ignoring the pain in my ribs:

'Smith – and his cronies – they said you'd had - to go to the office?'

'Yeah – that bastard Goffin came and told me there was a call from my Dad. They wanted me out of the way, they knew I'd make mincemeat of them if they tried it with me around! I'll beat them to a pulp, you see if I don't!' I put a hand on his arm:

'Not so fast, Jake. You'll only get in trouble. Wait – we'll get back at them, somehow.'

'Yeah… Okay. Come on, I'm taking you inside, we'll sit in the form room while you get over it.'

We were not supposed to be in the building during lunch, but I let him help me up the steps and along to our room, where I sat at my desk, breathing carefully. Jake perched on the edge of his, regarding me with a worried expression:

'Are you okay? Do you think they've broken anything?' I shook my head:

'I'll be fine! Just let me sit quiet for a bit, okay?'

We were still there when Mr Atkinson returned from his own lunch. He stopped in the doorway and took in the scene before speaking:

'You two – you aren't supposed to be here, you know?'

'Yes, sir – but Harry – Turner – fell over in the playground, and I thought he'd better sit down and rest for a while, sir. I hope that was right?' Atkinson nodded slowly:

'I think it probably was, Woodrow. Are you all right, Turner?' I looked up at him:

'Yes, sir, I'll be fine. I'm just winded, I think.'

'Hmmm… You could have gone to see Matron?'

'I didn't think it was serious enough to bother her, sir.' Jake spoke up.

'Hmm. All right – you may stay there until lessons begin, under the circumstances.' He sat at his desk, regarding us thoughtfully, then bent to mark the papers in front of him.

* * *

The next few days passed without incident. I'd felt much better by the time we went home that day, and hadn't said anything to my parents, although I'd had a good look at the fine selection of bruises on my chest, stomach and back that night before putting on my pyjamas. They soon faded.

Jake had been all for ambushing Smith and Pocock somewhere, giving them a taste of their own medicine; which, with his remarkable strength and my anger, the two of us could probably have done. But I persuaded him to leave it – I didn't want him getting into trouble on my account, any more than I wanted the same trouble for myself: Fighting, for any reason, was strictly prohibited at school, and we could have found ourselves in detention, or even caned, and it hardly seemed worth it, just to get revenge on them. And that would have been fine, if they hadn't decided to go for him as well...

He'd been on his guard, wondering if they'd try something; but by the time the weekend had passed, we both assumed that I'd been the prime target. After all, *I'd* been the one who started laughing at them, that morning. But the next Monday, without my noticing, all four of them sneaked out of the dining hall before the sweet was served. When I emerged into the sunshine, I found Jake sitting on the edge of the drain-box, hugging his chest, breathing as carefully as I had done a few days earlier.

'Jake!' He looked up:

'Bastards!' I sat next to him:

'Smith and Pocock?'

'Yeah. An' the other two.' He'd obviously put up a better struggle than I had – the knuckles of one hand were scraped and bleeding, as was his nose.

'You got one of them?' He chuckled, then drew a sharp breath at the pain in his ribs:

'Yeah! Pocock should 'ave a real shiner in a day or two!'

'Good for you! Now, come on.' I helped him to his feet.

'We can't go to the form room, Snoop'll guess something's going on?'

'You're going to Matron.'

'Don't be daft! She'll guess what's happened!'

'We'll tell her you fell off the box, right? Stick to that, she can't prove anything else.'

'But…'

'Stop arguing, and get a move on.'

He submitted, and let me lead him to her secluded den next to the school office. Mrs Parsons was just the kind of big, cheerful, kindly woman you always envisage as a school matron, even if she also had a tongue which could flay the skin from your back if you got on the wrong side of her. Now, she looked over Jake's injuries with a discerning eye:

'Fell off the old drain box, you say?'

'Yes, Matron' I confirmed.

'Aaah… Well, there's no real damage done, that I can see. Landed on your knuckles, did you, Woodrow?'

'That's right, Matron. And my nose.'

'I *see*… Very unfortunate! They'll heal up in a day or two, no doubt. And you hurt your ribs?'

'Just a bit, Matron.'

'Mmm. Well, you'll have to take things easy for a few days, understand?'

'Yes, Matron.'

'You'll keep an eye on him, will you, Turner?'

'Yes, Matron.'

She nodded, uncorking a bottle of Iodine, and dabbing a little on his scraped knuckles with a piece of cotton-wool. Another clean piece, dampened under the tap, to wipe away the blood from his nose:

'Go on, then. If the ribs are still painful in a day or two, come back and see me, Woodrow.'

'Yes, Matron.'

We made our escape, relieved that she hadn't seen through our ruse.

On our way home, on the bus, we set to discussing how to retaliate:

'We can't just let it go, now, Harry!'

'No, you're right. But what should we *do?* If we just beat them up, they'll do the same again, and it'll go on for *ever!'*

'Yeah, I know. There has to be a way of stopping them, once and for all...'

'Yeah – but *how?* Without getting ourselves into even more trouble than them?'

'If we could get *them* in real trouble, at school...'

'With the teachers, you mean?'

'Yeah... I've got an idea – we've got P.E. Wednesday, right?'

'Third period, you know that!'

'Yeah! Listen...'

Chapter Thirteen

'Hey – where's my tie-clip?' Smith also liked to think of himself as the form's dandy – among other things, he always wore a fancy clip on his school tie. We were all in the changing room, after our P.E. lesson, singlets and shorts discarded, taking out turns in the communal showers. Being what my mother would describe as well brought up, I always felt a little uncomfortable with the brief period of public nudity which this required; but this time, I glanced over at Jake, who was pulling on his underpants after exiting the shower and quickly drying himself. He returned a noncommittal smile, and went on dressing.

* * *

At the end of the lunch break, we all trooped back as usual into our form-room to collect our books for the next three periods. As we were variously sorting through our desks in search of the necessary text books, or mislaid homework, and chattering noisily, the warning hiss came from the desk nearest the door:

'Shhh! Snoop's coming!' Everything went quiet as Mr Atkinson swept into the room and strode up to his desk. He pulled out the chair, and went to sit down; but then he stopped, and bent to look closer at his seat. He put out a finger, and touched the surface of the wood – it came away sticky. His eyes lifted slowly to regard us all, his expression darkening:

'Stop right where you are, all of you!' Some of our classmates had been heading for the door; now, they halted in their tracks. It suited our purpose, that both Smith and Pocock happened to be among their number... Mr Atkinson bent down again, then reached to the floor as something caught his eye:

'What have we here?' He straightened up, a flash of gold twinkling in his hand: 'Smith! Is this yours, boy?'

'What, sir?'

'Don't 'what' me, come here and take a look!'

'Y-yes, sir.' Smith went up to him, his face full of trepidation.

'Well?' Smith's eyes went up to meet Mr Atkinson's, but he didn't reply.

'Is this yours?'

'Yes, sir.' His voice was barely audible.

'And *what* do you know about *this?'* Atkinson indicated his chair.

'What, sir?'

'Don't 'what' me, boy! This glue, on my chair?'

'Nothing, sir! I swear it!'

'So how does it come that your tie-clip is lying on the floor just here, Smith?' Now, the master's voice was deceptively quiet.

'I – I don't know, sir! I lost it, at P.E., this morning!'

'Did you indeed?'

'I did, sir! Everyone will tell you...' He looked around, but 'everyone' was being very discreet; only Pocock spoke:

'That's right, sir, he made ever such a fuss about it.'

Smith's face said that he was less than pleased at his friend's choice of words, but his relief was there in his expression as well.

'I see.' Mr Atkinson turned away to take another visual sweep of the area around his vandalised chair. He frowned, and then bent to reach into his waste bin:

'Well, well, what else do I spy?' He lifted out a soiled handkerchief and spread it out on the desktop, where everyone could see the monogrammed 'P' in one corner:

'This wouldn't *happen* to be yours, would it, Pocock?'

'No, sir! I mean…' He groped in his pocket, and a look of panic crossed his face: 'Oh…!'

Mr Atkinson stood there, the offending tie-clip and Pocock's handkerchief held one in each hand. He looked around the room, caught my eye for a moment, then swept his gaze on to rest on Jake for a second before returning it to the two boys in front of him:

'You two – Headmaster's office, *now!* The rest of you, go on to your class.' We all hurried out, eager to escape any further outpourings of our form-master's wrath.

* * *

We didn't see anything more of Smith or Pocock that afternoon. As we were all packing our things away, loading our bags with the night's homework, Mr Atkinson stood up from his newly-cleaned chair:

'Your two colleagues have been sent home for the afternoon in disgrace, for vandalising school property, to say nothing of attempting to affix their form-master permanently to his chair. They have also each received three strokes of the Headmaster's cane for their sins. Bear this in mind, should you be contemplating stepping out of line yourselves! Mr Turner – Mr Woodrow – I'd like a word with the two of you, before you go.'

We exchanged worried glances, but did as we were instructed and waited while our fellows made their exit, hurried on by Snoop's bellow:

'Go away, the rest of you, this is a private conversation!' He turned to us:

'Have either of you got anything to tell me?' We exchanged glances again before raising our eyes to him once more, shaking our heads:

'No, sir' we chorused, innocently. He regarded us steadily for a moment:

'Very well. You heard what I told the class. I am aware that both of you have suffered certain depredations at the hands of today's two culprits – I have taken it upon myself to have words with them, and make certain things clear, such as my dislike of any kind of bullying or rowdyism. You should not find yourselves in the line of fire in the future. Do you understand?'

'Yes, sir.' This time, our glances were puzzled, albeit also relieved.

'Very good, then. Get off home, both of you.' We turned to the door, only to be called back as I opened it:

'One thing more – if you two intend to make a career of organised crime, you'll need to find more subtle ways of framing other people for your misdemeanours! Now get out of here!'

We did as we were bid, before he could change his mind. But I swear I heard him chuckle as I closed the door.

Chapter Fourteen

We made it to the weekend without further incident. By then, Jake's injuries were no longer evident, and both of us were fully recovered; even Pocock's black eye was fading into insignificance.

Half term breaks then were not the full week that kids enjoy now – we had the weekend, of course, and the Bank Holiday Monday, and one additional day off on the Tuesday. I'd had little trouble persuading my mother to allow me to stay over at the lock cottage, but she had suggested a revised timetable:

'Why don't you go there for Monday and Tuesday, Hal? You could stay here Saturday, then – I think Dad would like that. I'm sure he misses you going in to work with him Saturday mornings the way you used to.'

'Yes, all right – I'll see if that's okay with Jake and his Dad.'

While we were still in Oxford, it had been something of a tradition for Dad to take me in to the factory with him on Saturdays. He was usually busy, doing paperwork in his office mostly, but I was allowed to wander around the workshop itself, talking to the men and watching them at the lathes or the milling machines, trying my hand at simpler jobs under their watchful eyes. What today's Health and Safety regulations would make of that, I dread to think! So that Saturday, I went with him for the first time in a couple of months; I was delighted when the men there welcomed me like a long-lost friend, and the foreman, old Henry Payne, insisted I help him with a bit of fancy machining on a special job he had to finish.

Jake turned up on the Sunday afternoon – I hadn't been expecting him, but he'd decided to come over and see if I was at home. We went for a walk around the village – I think he was still nervous of my father's reaction to him, then – or at least, he walked for a time while I scooted along with him on my bike as we chatted about everything and nothing. Then a thought struck me:

'You haven't got a bike, have you?'

'Nah – not now. We had one, when we were on the boat.'

'So you can ride one?'

''Course!'

'D'you want a go?'

'Can I?'

''Course!'

So we changed places. I walked, while Jake rode up and down the village main street, passing me, turning, passing me again, and so on. The pleasure on his face was clear; at last, he reined it in, and sat scooting along at my side as I had been doing before:

'Thanks, Harry – that was great!'

'Why don't you have your own bike, now?'

'Wouldn't be much good, over the track to the lock, would it?'

'No, I s'pose not. But you could use it on the towpath, couldn't you?'

'Yeah… That's what we used to do, ride ahead to set the locks ready for the boat. No need for that, now – but it would be quicker, to get to Slat Mill, or Bourton, wouldn't it? Maybe I'll suggest it to Dad…'

I let him stay on the bike for the rest of the time, until we made our way back to my house. He'd said he had to be home by six, for dinner, but his time-keeping also relied upon me – he didn't have a wristwatch, either. It might sound as though I am making much of the differences in our state of wealth, but it is only with hindsight that they seem at all significant – at the time, neither of us set any real store by them, though I suspect Jake was more aware of them than I was, remembering his early wariness of my friendly advances.

We parted at the garden gate, just before half past five, reiterating our agreement for me to turn up at Burdon Lock the following morning, with my overnight bag.

* * *

I got there about nine o'clock, after the half-hour walk across the fields. I was getting well used to the journey, now, almost as familiar with the territory as Jake, stepping over the rougher parts of the path without a second thought. He was in the garden when I arrived, weeding the vegetables; I dropped my bag in the kitchen, and set out to help without a thought. My mother would have had a shock, could she have seen – she had long ago given up trying to interest me in helping her in our own garden!

We spent the Monday in an assortment of tasks for Ernie Woodrow, part of it down at Bourton Lock, the next one

South of Burdon, freeing off and greasing the paddle gear, a delightfully mucky job for two schoolboys to be entrusted with! By the evening, my shirt and trousers were pleasingly grubby, and I was deliciously tired. The weather had been fine and dry, if rather overcast – that night's forecast on the radio suggested warm sunshine for the following day.

Dinner that night was an enormous and succulent casserole, with big, fluffy dumplings and wonderfully tender pieces of stewing steak lurking among the home-grown vegetables:

'You two've bin a great 'elp today, lads – 'Ow d'yer fancy 'aving tomorrer off?'

'Can we, Mr Woodrow?'

'That'd be brilliant, Dad!'

'Yeah, well – the weather's set foine. I thought yer might loike to take a picnic, goo off in the country, maybe?'

'That would be great, if you don't mind?'

''Course Oi don't, boy! I knoo Jacob 'ere doon't get enough toime to 'imself, 'n Oi can manage on me own, for one day. Now, would yer loike a bath, 'fore yeh goo to bed? Yeh mus' be 'ot 'n sweaty after the day yeh've put in?'

'Er – no, it's all right, I'm okay, really!' I knew that their bath was an iron tub, which was set up in front of the range when required; and I've already mentioned my ingrained boyish modesty. But Jake laughed:

'Harry's a bit worried about taking his clothes off, Dad!'

'Oh! Roight – well, that's noo problem, boy. Oi can fill yer a tub, then me 'n Jake'll goo in the sittin' room 'n leave you to it. 'Ow'd that be?'

'That would be fine, if you're sure it's all right?'

''Course 'tis, boy! You gettin' in after 'Arry, Jake?'

'Yes, Oi will, Dad. Oi'm 'ot 'n sticky, too.' My friend's sudden lapses into his old boater's idiom still caught me by surprise from time to time – mostly, when I was with him, he'd speak with the acquired tones of the town, even in front of his father.

Soaking in the hot tub, beside the still-warm range, was a wonderful feeling. It felt rather strange, maybe, to be having a bath in the kitchen, after the luxury of our clean, tiled bathroom, but perhaps that was part of its appeal. Ernie Woodrow had retired to his sitting room after filling the tub from an enormous kettle, heated over the range, and topping it off with water from the tap over the sink to reach a comfortable temperature. Jake had gone up to his bedroom, preparatory to jumping in when I got out.

It felt so good, that I was in no hurry to do that. So much so, that he came down again while I was still soaking, walking in with only a towel around his middle and a grin on his face:

'You still in there, Harry? Come on, it's my turn now!'

'Go away then, and I'll get out!'

'Oh, don't be so daft! We've been in the showers often enough – here, have my towel.' He peeled it off, handed it to me; I carefully looked the other way as I took it, then stood up, quickly covering myself as I did so. I stepped out of the tub, and he took my place, settling into the still-warm water with a satisfied sigh. I dried myself, keeping my back to him, and then delved into my bag for some clean clothes:

'Should I put my pyjamas on now?'

'No, not yet – I want to go outside for a while.'

'Oh – okay.' I slipped on a clean pair of pants, a fresh shirt, and risked a glance around as I began to do up the buttons. Jake looked up – there was a devilish twinkle in his blue eyes:

'I know where I'll take you tomorrow, especially if the weather's as good as they said!'

'Where's that?'

'Ah! You wait and see!'

Fully dressed again, I went to join Ernie Woodrow in the sitting room:

'Sit down, boy – feelin' better noo, are yeh?'

'Much better, thank you, Mr Woodrow.'

'Aye, good. 'Arry?'

'Yes, Mr Woodrow?' He paused, looking at me thoughtfully for a moment, then went on:

'Me 'n Jake – our way of loife's different from yours, boy. Oi hope that won't get in the way of the two of yeh? 'E thinks the world of you – yer the first real friend 'e's 'ad, 'specially since we coom off the boat. Yer see – when yeh live in close quarters, loike we did then, yer can't *afford* ter be fussy 'bout things. If 'e's not bothered 'bout people 'e knows, loike you, seein' 'im wi' no clothes on, it's not 'cause he's bein' *rude,* see?'

'Yes, I understand. I know we're not the same, in lots of ways – but we're *friends.* That's what matters, isn't it?' He smiled at me:

'Yeah, that's roight. Yer a good lad, 'Arry.'

We settled into a companionable silence for a few minutes, until Jake, freshly scrubbed and dressed in a pair of well-worn trousers and a clean if threadbare shirt, came to join us. For a while, we talked; mostly, Ernie Woodrow sat reminiscing about his days on the boats, from his own childhood until they'd had to give it up. I listened, spellbound; Jake would put in an occasional comment, backing up his father's story, explaining things I might have missed. Dusk began to fall; Ernie fell silent, the particular memory he'd been sharing concluded; Jake got up from his chair:

'Let's go out for bit, Harry.'

'Where're we going?'

'Oh – just outside. Come on.' Slightly puzzled, I got up and followed him out onto the lockside; we strolled along, not talking, up to the top gate, where he stepped over the balance beam and sat on it, gazing out along the straight length of the canal which led away to the North, out of sight under Burdon Bridge, and then through Slat Mill Lock and on towards Napton, where the Oxford Canal joined the Grand Union. The skies had cleared; I sat with him, keeping quiet, aware of a mood in my friend that I hadn't seen before. He said nothing for a time, then glanced quickly at me before returning his eyes Northwards:

'I come out here every night.'

His voice was soft, contemplative – I held my silence, feeling that to say anything would be out of place. He glanced up at the sky, where scattered clouds were glowing pink and gold with the sunset among a scattering of early stars, then down again to its reflection in the still water:

'It's beautiful, isn't it?' Still, I felt he didn't need me to answer. He went on, musingly: 'Especially on a night like this, when it's so bright and clear – you can sit and watch the stars come out. I love to be here, on my own – Dad'll be sat in his armchair, with his pipe. I love this place,

Summer or Winter, in the dark, in the rain; or like this…'

He fell silent for a moment: 'This is where I belong, Harry. This is my *world*. I don't fit, not really, anywhere else. What's going to happen to me? What am I going to *do?* I don't want to work on the bank, in a factory, or an office, or…' he shrugged, and fell silent again. I wanted to say something, something to ease his discomfort, to give him peace of mind, but still I felt constrained, unwilling to shatter the moment.

Overhead, the sky gradually darkened, the pinks and golds fading, turning to ever-deepening blues as night closed in around us. More stars began to emerge, their reflections twinkling in the polished mirror of the still canal; I can still remember my sense of wonder, as I contemplated the true beauty of nature for perhaps the first time in my young life, suddenly understanding, sharing my friend's desire to stay here forever, to not let the outside world intrude upon something which seemed so complete, so *right*.

At last, he broke the silence:

'Perhaps I won't have to worry about it.' His words, something in his tone, disturbed me:

'What d'you mean, Jake?' In the near-darkness, I felt rather than saw his face turn to me, felt rather than saw his shrug, his self-conscious smile:

'Maybe I won't live that long.'

'Don't say things like that! Don't even *think* it!' I was shaken, not only by such an idea of mortality but by his calm acceptance of it.

'Oh, come on, Harry – people *die,* sometimes – look at my Mum.'

'That's different!'

'Is it? *Kids* die too, sometimes. I know people, boaters, who've had kids die.' I had no answer to this; my thoughts went back to the source of his introspection:

'Pr'aps – when we're grown up – we could get a boat? The two of us, we could manage a *pair,* even, couldn't we?' His smile grew wider with a sudden return of his usual self-confidence:

'Yeah – maybe we could, at that… Come on, let's go back indoors, it's getting cold out here. And you've got some exercise coming, tomorrow!'

'I have?' He just grinned as he rose to his feet.

Chapter Fifteen

The next morning, I was awake just after seven. Perhaps it was Jake's movements that had aroused me – he was already up, and getting dressed, as I rolled over and rubbed the sleep from my eyes:

'Hi, Harry! All right?'

'Yeah – you?'

'Fine! It's a lovely mornin', look!' I followed his gesture – sunshine was streaming in through the window, brightening the plain but comfortable room, rim-lighting his tousled hair and tanned shoulders. He finished dressing, looked around again:

'Come on, get up! I'll go 'n put the kettle on.' I threw back the sheets and swung my legs to the floor as he left the room and thundered down the stairs.

The previous night, as we got ready for bed, he'd shown me his pet project. In the surprisingly-large bedroom, a battered old chest of drawers stood four-square below the window, between the two ill-matched single beds – his father had already thrown a spare sheet and blanket over the one I was to use – and on its top, among a scattering of small tools and scraps of wood, lay an almost-completed model of a motor narrowboat. Jake proudly showed me how he'd constructed it, just like the real thing, with its miniature ribs and knees, long planks for the hull steamed and curved to shape. It lacked any paint on the cabin, and he was in the process of making the running gear – deck-board and cratch, stands and planks. I duly admired it, wishing that I had the skill and the patience to do something similar.

After going back indoors, we had sat talking with his father again for a while, over big mugs of hot chocolate. At home, I was expected to be in bed by nine at the latest, so to be still up, chatting, listening to their conversation, at such a late hour, was quite a treat. It was almost eleven o'clock when Jake's father finally chased us off to bed, complaining jocularly that *he* had work to do the next day even if we didn't!

* * *

By half past eight, we were ready to set off on our still-unexplained expedition, full of boiled eggs and strong tea, with a big pack of crusty bread and Ernie's usual aggressive cheddar, and a couple of apples apiece. Jake also carried a big old Thermos flask, filled with more creosote-coloured tea.

But our departure was delayed a little: We were just setting off, in the direction of the bridge, when an animal appeared through the arch – a *horse!* Moments later, as it drew closer, Jake corrected my first impression:

'That's Dolly!' He turned to me, a delighted grin on his face: 'Joe Skinner's ole mule – the *Friendship* must be comin'!' And true enough, as he spoke the fore-end of a deep-loaded boat appeared in the bridge. We stood and waited, while mule and boat drew steadily closer, then

Jake dashed back into the house, to emerge moments later with his windlass in his hand. He quickly drew the top paddles; I leant against the balance beam, eased the gate open when the weight of the water came off it, as I had learnt to do. The mule clopped past me without so much as a sideways glance, and came to a halt, with no word of command, at the far end of the lock.

The boat, more brightly painted than any I had so far seen, slipped noiselessly past me; a man with a bushy walrus moustache, an old trilby hat pulled low over his eyes, stepped off with a windlass as his wife dropped a heavy rope around the end-post of the gate, pulling it to and stopping the boat at the same time.

'Thank ye, Jake.' The man's voice was rather high-pitched, his accent different from other boaters I'd met, with the soft round tones of rural Oxfordshire to the fore; he glanced across the lock to where my friend was dropping the paddle, while he did the same on my side.

'Joe – this's 'Arry, 'Arry Turner.' The man turned to me:

'Ow d'yer do - Joe Skinner, 'n that's Rose' he waved towards his wife, who was stood in the hatches at the back of the cabin.

'Hello, Mr Skinner, pleased to meet you.' He nodded, a smile crinkling the bright blue eyes which fixed me good-humouredly from below the shade of his hat-brim, giving them a roguish sparkle, and hurried down the lockside to raise a bottom paddle.

'Kettle's on – got toime fer a cuppa?' Rose addressed Jake as he went to follow suit on the far side. He looked back over his shoulder, glanced enquiringly at me; I nodded my eager acquiescence, and he said:

'Yeah, please, Rose!' She smiled and ducked down into the cabin. The lock emptied, Jake and I swung the gates; Dolly set off, again with no visible prompting from anyone, took up the slack and began to pull the boat out. Joe whistled her to a halt as the boat emerged from the lock-tail, and dropped a rope around a bollard to hold it against the bank. Our bags and flask still lay on the lockside – Ernie gave us all a wave from the cottage door, where he had watched the whole operation, and wandered down to join us.

We each drained a big mug of Rose's tea, which was, if anything, even stronger than Ernie Woodrow's, standing beside the boat's cabin; Joe leant on the cabin-top, swapping news with Jake and his father. I held my silence, slightly in awe of the man – he was, if not exactly tall, quite an imposing figure, with broad shoulders apparent under his old jacket. Even on such a mild morning, he wore a muffler crossed around his neck; the brim of his hat was turned down all round, shading those bright, twinkling eyes – my impression was of a man who, while friendly enough, was economical with words. Rose, by contrast, was quite slightly built, very different from the buxom bulk of Betty Shine or her daughter; a red beret held her greying hair in check.

Jake turned to me, reminded me that Joe was what he called a 'number one' – he owned the *Friendship,* working for himself rather than for one of the carrying companies. We handed our empty mugs back to Rose - the old couple waved their farewells as Joe clicked his tongue at Dolly to set her on her way once more. I've called them old, but in fact I would have had difficulty in guessing their ages –

both had the typical boater's complexion, weatherbeaten, creased but somehow ageless. I can still remember my feelings as I watched them go on their way - a sense of great respect for them, a feeling that they somehow epitomised the proud, private people of the waterways.

We collected our bags and, rather belatedly, set off on our way. Jake still wouldn't tell me where he was taking me, except that 'We're goin' up into the hills beyond the railway. Don't worry, you'll like it there!'

We duly crossed the lines at the level crossing, and headed on along the bridleway. The ground rose steadily; at last, he turned off the worn track, heading along the edge of a field where there didn't seem to be any proper path. I just tagged along, reasoning that he clearly knew where he was going; he led us further up, beyond the cultivated fields, onto the top of a little range of low hills. We breasted a slight rise; he turned to me in triumph:

'There! What d'you think?' Nestling between the hilltops was a pond – a small lake might be a better description, the kind that might be called a Tarn in the Northern counties. I stepped cautiously up to the edge; the water was astonishingly clear, allowing me to see a sandy bottom which gave way to a jumble of smoothed boulders farther out. It might have been a hundred yards or more long, but no more than about sixty wide:

'It gets deep in the middle, but the water's still so clear you can see the bottom if you duck your head under, Harry!' I looked up, gazed around:

'Yeah – it's great, Jake!'

'Let's have a bite, then we can go in!'

'Go in?'

'For a swim, of course!'

'Swim? We haven't got any costumes!' Jake gave a conspiratorial laugh:

'No!'

'So…?'

'Who needs a costume? No-one else ever comes here, Harry! And it's so warm in the sun…'

'But…'

'Come on, let's eat first.' He sat down on the grass, opened his bag and broke off a big hunk of bread. Taking a bite, he unwrapped the cheese and took a bite of that, too. I sat beside him, and opened my own lunch – I was hungry, after the trek up there, and ate about half of my own bread and cheese; we washed it down with a swig of tea each, sharing the plastic cup from the top of the flask, and munched on an apple apiece. He packed the remnants away in his bag, and bent to take off his shoes and socks:

'You really want to go swimming?'

'Sure! Don't you?'

'But…' The water did look rather inviting, so clear and fresh, and I was quite hot after our long walk; the sun was very warm, too, and I found myself sorely tempted. I wasn't a strong swimmer, though, and the idea of going naked in front of my friend went against all I'd been taught. I sat back and watched as Jake got to his feet, unbuttoned and threw off his shirt, then went to release his belt. He paused, looking down at me:

'Harry – we've had to strip off in the showers, no end of times, haven't we? Like I said, no-one else ever comes here, no-one's going to see!'

'Yeah, but – in the showers…'

'That's different, right? *Why's* it different, Harry? Come on, try it – the water here's fantastic, it's lovely and cool, you'll love it, really!' I still hesitated, tempted but embarrassed; he chuckled, carried on undoing his trousers:

'*I'm* going in, anyway! You can wait there, if you're too scared!' He knew that taunt would goad me into action, even against my better judgement – I quickly whipped off my own shoes and socks, threw off my shirt, dropped my trousers and pants before I could think better of it. I ran over to the bank and leapt into the water even before Jake did; he stood there, hands on his hips, a big grin on his face as I rose to the surface again, spluttering and gasping – the water had been colder than I had anticipated. The next moment, he was beside me, laughing, splashing water over me, swimming off as I tried to chase after him. He was much quicker, stronger than I was; realising he'd left me struggling in his wake, he turned back:

'You okay, Harry?'

'Yeah, sure! I'm not so good a swimmer as you!' The next couple of hours became a kind of combined coaching session and hilarious romp – by the time we both dragged ourselves out, tired but still laughing, onto the bank, for another attack on our lunch-bags, it actually came as a surprise to me to remember that I hadn't got anything on. We sat in the sun, letting its warmth dry our skin, tucking in to the rest of our bread and cheese, taking turns to drink from the cup, until we felt as wonderfully full as we were tired. Jake rolled over onto his tummy, propping his chin on his hands, elbows braced on the grass; I followed suit, enjoying the heat of the sun on my bare back. We lay in silence for a while; then Jake flashed a glance at me:

'Harry?'

'Yeah?'

'What you said last night?'

'What?'

'About us going on the boats?'

'Yeah?'

'Did you mean it?' I looked across at him, surprised at the question:

''Course!'

'You really fancy working on the cut? With me?' I rolled onto my side, facing him:

'Why not?' He raised himself on one elbow, looking at me:

'Yeah... Why not? It'd be brilliant, wouldn't it?'

'Yeah!' I turned face-down again, resting my head on my crossed arms. Silence reigned again for a while, until he said:

'My Dad reckons the cut's dying.'

'What d'you mean?'

'He says there's less and less trade, fewer and fewer orders, ever since the end of the war. So maybe there won't be any jobs for us, by the time we're old enough.'

'Well – perhaps he's wrong? Maybe things'll get better again? After all, everything's supposed to be getting better now, isn't it, now rationing's finished and all that. That's what my Dad says, anyway!'

'Yeah – and he runs a business, so he should know, shouldn't he?'

'I reckon so.'

'But – *my* Dad says they're trying to *close* the cut, down to Oxford. It can't get better, if there's no canal *there,* can it?' This jerked me out of my semi-stupor:

'*Close* it?'

'Yeah.'

'But they can't just *close* it, just like that, can they?'

'Dunno. Maybe they can, if they want to.'

'But – what will you and your Dad do, if that happens?'

'Oh, they're not on about closing our bit, only from Banbury. There's too much trade on our end – but maybe that'll stop too, one day.'

'Well, we'll have to make sure it *doesn't!* If we get our own boats, we can make sure that we keep working, can't we? Then, they won't be able to shut it!'

'Yeah…'

Flawed schoolboy logic, perhaps – but it made sense to us, at the time. We lapsed into silence again, until our bodies were dry, and then spoiled that result by diving back into the tarn for another swim. So we had to lie in the sun for a while again, to dry – we drained off the last of the tea, slowly, reluctantly put our clothes on again, and at last made our weary way back across the fields, along the bridleway, over the level crossing and so to the cottage in time for another of Ernie Woodrow's superb casseroles.

Chapter Sixteen

It was over that meal that Jake cautiously probed his father about the future of the canal. We were tucking in with some relish when he broached the subject:

'Dad?'

'Yes, Jake?'

'You think they might really close the cut down to Oxford?' Ernie swallowed his mouthful, raised his eyes to his son:

''Oo knows, lad. Oi 'ope not.'

'Boot they moight?'

'There's talk of it. They say there's no traffic on it, so it moight as well not be there. Clayton's 'ave stopped the traffic from h'Oxford ter Banbury, now the ol' gas works boy the river's closed down; that's whoy Alby Beechey's runnin' this length, from Leamington ter Banbury. Boot - ' he waved his fork at us across the table: 'there's ter be a big meetin' about it, in a week or two's toime. Protest meetin', in the Town 'All in h'Oxford. That poet feller from the 'Versity's in charge of it, soo Oi 'ear.'

'Are you going, Mr Woodrow?' I asked; he grinned at me:

'Oo-aar, boy! Oi'm a-gooin' fer sure! Oi want to know what's gooin' ter 'appen; 'n mebbe Oi'll put in moy two-pen'orth, as well!'

'Good fer you, Dad!' Ernie's grin turned to Jake:

'Well, Oi can't joost sit back 'n let it 'appen, can Oi? 'Oo knows, it moight be this length next, if the loads to Banbury drop off. 'N yer can still get through ter h'Oxford – all it needs is soomone ter start sendin' loads all the way.' He waved the fork again for emphasis: 'The Brew'ry 'ave said as they'd still 'ave coal by boat, or so Oi 'ear; there's a new feller, bought an old Grand Union motor, startin' doin' regular deliveries fer 'em, now.'

'What 'bout oother jobs, Dad?'

'Well, could be, lad. If one comp'ny's started it, oothers moight follow.' Jake flashed a glance at me, hope twinkling in his eyes as his father went on: 'There's bin talk of a big rally in Banbury, to campaign for the cut teh be kep' open. On the Bank 'Oliday in August, Oi think it is. They do say as Leslie Morton's be'ind it.' Jake leaned over to explain to me:

'Leslie Morton's the man who runs Willow Wren.' Neither of us mentioned our still-vague ideas of becoming boaters when we left school; the talk drifted to other subjects until we'd finished eating. I stopped to help with the washing up, then reluctantly packed my bag and headed for home, Ernie's insistence that I 'coom 'n stop agen soon!' ringing in my ears.

* * *

The meeting Ernie Woodrow had been talking about took place on the third of June. Oxford's Town Hall, in St Aldate's, is a hugely impressive building; its cavernous interior was well filled that night, when my father and I walked in. I'd persuaded him to go, and take me along – although not particularly involved with the canal, I think he felt that to lose it would be a bad move, a loss of our industrial heritage if nothing else. We squeezed into seats near the back, and listened intently to the prolonged discussions, ably overseen by John Betjeman. Arguments went back and forth, and feelings ran high a few times; it was late on, when Mr Betjeman waved to acknowledge a speaker on the far side of the hall from us, and a familiar figure pushed himself to his feet:

'Ernest Woodrow, Mister Chairman. Oi'm lock-keeper at Burdon Leigh – that's a bit North o' Banbury - 'n Oi'd loike ter say that it's moy view that this cut should stay open. There's still quoite a lot o' boats travel moy length, to Banbury, fer the Co-op, 'n the Gas Works, among oother places, 'n they could still carry coal 'n oother goods roight inter h'Oxford, if anyone 'ad the sense ter use 'em. The cut's still okay – Clayton's 'ave only joost stopped the traffic from the old gas-works teh the tar distillery at Banbury, and Oi've 'eard that Colonel Morrell's let a contract for reg'lar loads o' coal from Coventry, now. So they can't say there's no trade, can they? 'N we've bin told 'ow mooch it would cost to shut it, 'n fill it in – what Oi say is, whoy waste that mooney? Let's get some more trade back, 'n 'ave the Transport Commission spend their mooney *drudgin'* the booger out, so's the boats can carry to their proper capacity!'

In the round of scattered applause that greeted his words, I nudged my father and pointed: 'That's Jake's father, Dad! He said he was coming tonight!' He smiled down at me, nodding his understanding. Ernie was still on his feet, uncharacteristically dressed in black trousers, a brilliantly white shirt and a plain brown waistcoat, a slightly tired looking trilby hat on his head:

'There's talk of a stroike on the railways, as you'll all 'ave 'eard. So – it makes sense, doosn't it, ter keep the canal open? Then, the boats can 'elp out if that goos ahead. Don't let's 'ave all our eggs in oone basket, that's what Oi say!'

More applause echoed as he sat down, Mr Betjeman nodding his agreement with the sentiments.

It was getting quite late when the meeting finally broke up. To judge from the chatter I overheard as we made our way out, people seemed to feel that it had been a success, if only in demonstrating the level of popular resistance to the proposed closure; on the front steps, I caught sight of Ernie Woodrow, and dragged my father over to meet him:

'Dad – this is Mr Woodrow, Jake's father.' Ernie turned as I took hold of his sleeve – the full one: 'Mr Woodrow – I'd like you to meet my father.' He gave me a broad smile, held out his hand:

'Mr Turner – pleased ter meet yer! 'Arry's told us a lot about you.'

'Good to meet you too, Mr Woodrow. I hope Harry doesn't make a nuisance of himself, coming to your house so often?'

'Noo, goodness me, 'e's alwes welcome! 'E's good coomp'ny fer moy lad, 'n 'e 'elps out noo end wi' the chores, too.'

'How did you get here, Mr Woodrow?' I asked.

'Boy train, 'Arry.' He pulled his old fob watch out of

his waistcoat pocket: ''N if yeh'll forgive me, Oi'd better 'urry else oi'll miss the las' one back!'

'How far does the train take you, Mr Woodrow?' Dad asked him.

'Ernie, please! Joost ter Banbury; Oi can walk the last little bit from there.' Dad glanced down at me:

'We can't let you do that, at this time of night! I can give you a lift to Burdon Leigh, that's got to be much easier for you, surely? And it's Teddy, right?'

'That's very generous of yeh – if yer sure it's noo trouble, it would save me a bit of an 'ike!'

'Come on, then, the car's just down here.'

The two men sat in the front seat, relegating me to the back for the journey. I didn't mind at all – I was delighted that they seemed to be getting along well, discussing the pros and cons of canal carrying and the prospects of keeping the Oxford Canal open all the way home, and quietly hoping that this might improve my father's impression of Jake. At the house, Dad invited Mr Woodrow in for a drink; they continued their chat in the sitting-room while I was despatched off to bed.

I lay awake for a while, long enough to hear my father seeing Ernie off for his walk back to the lock, happy at what I'd heard that night – it sounded as though the canal would probably stay open, if the powers that were took any notice of the strength of feeling expressed. And therefore, maybe Jake and I *would* be able to have our boats, one day – carrying coal for Morrell's Brewery, almost past our front door – wouldn't *that* be great…?

Chapter Seventeen

The next few weeks were a time of growing excitement for me. My birthday falls in late June, and that year I felt its approach with typical boyish anticipation. I would be twelve – a bit too old, maybe, for a little-kid type party, but my parents had promised to bring my old friends from Oxford over to see me, and our new home.

During that time, Jake and I spent a lot of our free time together talking about our plans to be boaters when we grew up, our enthusiasm bolstered after the apparently unanimous rejection of the canal's closure by the meeting. At school, things were quiet – somehow, the story had gone around that the first-year's trainee bullies' punishment and disgrace had been brought about by our manipulations, and the two of us were, for a time at least, treated generally with a kind of wary admiration. Smith and Pocock themselves were giving us a wide berth – I suspect Snoop's 'words' with them had been extremely pointed and emphatic – even if their snobbish disregard for my friend was undiminished.

The promised rail strike had come to pass, the footplatemen downing tools in pursuit of a better deal from British Railways; but its hoped-for effect on canal trade had fizzled out:

'Noo-one's got any spare boats, or crews, yeh see. Oi

'ear as there've bin noo end o' people callin' Barlow's 'n
the others, lookin' fer deliv'ries – they've taken all they
can, they're workin' flat out, all the boaters, boot they can't
'andle any more!' So Jake's father explained it to us, on
one of my regular Saturday visits. I was usually expected
to stop for the evening meal, now – Jake would drop in
after school for a sandwich and tea with my mother and I,
once or twice a week, but he had resisted all attempts to
get him to join us for a proper meal again.

* * *

When my birthday finally arrived, I awoke early to find
the anticipated heap of presents by the end of my bed.
There were things like Summer clothes and books from
aunts, uncles and grandparents, cards from all and sundry,
one or two of them with pound notes tucked inside, but
pride of place went to a huge box labelled 'with love
from Mum and Dad'. Inside, I was enthralled and
delighted to find a real flying model of a Spitfire, complete
with a proper, albeit single-cylinder, petrol engine. Radio
control was almost unheard of then – this one had control
lines which attached to either wing, so you flew it in a
circle around yourself, making it climb or descend by
twisting your wrist. I couldn't wait to try it, but school,
sadly, intervened.

As we settled into our seats on the bus that morning,
Jake turned to me:

'Birthday boy, then?' I grinned:

'Yeah! I'm as old as you, now!'

'Hah! Not for long, kid!'

'All right, Grandad!' He gave me a playful cuff around the ear; I retaliated, and we earned ourselves another reproachful gaze from the driver. I hadn't expected anything more from him – I knew my old friends from Oxford would probably bring me some small presents when they came to see me, but he and his father didn't have the spare money to waste buying me anything. The day passed, like any other school day; I had already persuaded him to stop in for tea that evening, and while my mother was cutting the sandwiches and boiling the kettle, we took the Spitfire out into the pasture field behind the house. My father had shown me how to fill its petrol tank and start the engine before breakfast, receiving a glare from Mum for his pains, so now we got it flying for the first time, although we had barely time for a quick go apiece before we were called in for tea.

* * *

That weekend, I went to the lock cottage as usual. Dad and I had given the Spitfire a good outing every night, using the long summer evenings to their best advantage; Nicky's father was going to bring him and my other friend Max over for the afternoon on Sunday, when Mum had a special tea planned for us. The Saturday wasn't out of the ordinary, until the evening; Jake and I did the expected round of odd jobs to help his father, and then spent much of the afternoon kicking a ball around in the field behind the cottage. But after dinner, Ernie Woodrow produced a birthday cake from the pantry, a huge grin on his face as he placed it ceremoniously on the table in front of me.

He'd obviously made it himself – it was a little lop-sided, and heavy with chocolate icing; there was even a single candle stuck in the middle, which he lit, apologising that he didn't have the other eleven. I duly blew it out, to his encouraging 'Goo on, 'Arry, make a wish!'

We tucked in to a big slice each – it was, to be frank, a bit stodgy, but then I don't imagine he'd had a lot of practice at baking cakes. The two of them insisted on singing 'Happy Birthday' - a moderately excruciating experience - and then Jake got up and left the room. Moments later, he was back; he handed me a long, thin package untidily bundled in newspaper:

'Happy birthday, Harry. Sorry it's not in proper paper, but… you understand.'

'Of course…' Puzzled, I carefully unwrapped it, to find myself holding the now-finished model boat he'd so proudly shown me a few weeks before. I looked up at him, dumbfounded:

'But…?'

'It's for you, Harry. Happy birthday' he repeated.

'I can't take *this,* Jake! It's yours, you've spent *ages* making it…!'

''Course you can! Look at the name on the side!' I looked; the miniature cabinsides were now beautifully painted, with red panels and dark green borders, and the legend 'Henry Turner, Canal Carrier' carefully signwritten in white. Still astonished, unconvinced, I tried to protest again, but he stopped me:

'Listen – I've had all the fun of building it, and now I want *you* to have it, all right? I'm going to start building the butty, next – then, we'll have our pair, right? It's a…

a promise, of the real ones we're going to run, one day, okay?'

'Okay…' I acquiesced, feeling deeply affected by his generosity. Ernie had watched all this, a wide smile on his round, creased face; now, he reached behind him to the old dresser, pulled out three bottles from its dark recesses:

'Toime for a celebrat'ry drink, boys!' He uncapped the bottles, poured the dark brown contents into three mis-matched glasses, handed one to each of us: ''Ere's teh you, 'Arry – long loife 'n 'appiness, boy.' We clinked our glasses together, as Jake echoed: 'To you, Harry – happy birthday!' The strong, dark beer was quite bitter – I'd had the odd taste of my father's drinks occasionally, but this was the first time I'd been given a glass to myself. At first, I was almost forcing it down; but by the time the glass was half-empty, I found myself rather enjoying it. As we drank, Ernie sat listening to our eager plans for the future; we hadn't told him previously of our decision to become boaters when we left school, and now he heard us out, nodding in sympathetic understanding, interjecting the odd comment or word of advice along the way. At the end, when our enthusiasm began to run down, he said:

'Good look to yeh – Oi 'ope it all works out! 'N mebbe yeh could foind room fer an old one-armed butty-steerer in yer crew?' Jake and I looked at each other – we hadn't thought of that:

''Course we can, Dad!' He got up and went to put an arm around his father's shoulders: 'Can't we, Harry?'

'We wouldn't go without you, Mr Woodrow!' He beckoned me over; I stood up and went to him, and he slipped his arm around my waist, looking proudly from me to his son and back again:

'Oi couldn't wish fer a better son, or a better friend, than you two, could Oi?' My heart swelled, to be addressed as 'friend', treated like an equal, by a grown-up, especially one for whom I had such respect and affection.

That day, their simple celebration and unpretentious joy at sharing my birthday, remains with me as one of the happiest moments of my life.

Chapter Eighteen

Sunday dawned bright and sunny – we didn't know it then, but that year was to bring us a prolonged heat-wave. Jake had insisted on walking home with me the previous evening; more used to the occasional glass of beer than I was, he had, I think, decided that he ought to escort me to ensure my safe arrival. I carried the boat, carefully re-wrapped in newspaper; at our gate, he refused my invitation to come in for a while, saying he should get back to his Dad.

'But you are coming tomorrow, aren't you? For tea, with my old friends from Oxford?' He held my eyes for a moment, his expression serious:

'No, Harry. Thank you for asking me – but that's your time with them, and your own family. We've had our party today, haven't we?'

'Oh, please, Jake! It won't be right, without you there!' He shook his head:

'You'll have a good time, with the others, you don't need me there too. And anyway... I wouldn't fit in, would I?'

I went to protest again, but he hushed me: 'We've had a great time, today, haven't we? I'm sorry it wasn't more... Oh, you know! But, I enjoyed it, and I hope you did too. I'll see you at school, Monday, right?'

Upset, still, and disappointed, I gave in; he turned to go:

'Jake?'

'Yeah?' He looked back over his shoulder.

'Thank you, for the boat – it's absolutely brilliant!' He grinned:

'I'm glad you like it, Harry – just wait 'til we get our real ones! We'll have 'Turner and Woodrow, Canal Carriers' on the side, then!'

'Or 'Woodrow and Turner' – you'll be captain, you know most about boating.'

'We'll see!' With a shrug of his shoulders, and a last cheerful grin, he set off for home. I let myself in – no-one locked their doors then, especially in such a small community – to find my father sitting at the dining room table with his cigarette, while my mother bustled in the kitchen after their late dinner:

'Hello, Dad!' He smiled up at me:

'Hi, Harry – had a good day?'

'Yeah! Jake's Dad made a cake for me – we had it after dinner; he even put a candle on it!' His smile grew wider:

'Did they sing you 'Happy Birthday', too?'

'Yeah – it was pretty awful! But – you know!' He laughed at my pained expression:

'It's the thought that counts, Harry! What've you got there?' He gestured with his cigarette to the package under my arm. I set it carefully down on the table, unwrapping it to show him:

'My present from Jake, Dad – Isn't it super?' He bent forward to take a closer look; I demonstrated how the stands and planks could be removed, just like the real thing, along with the deck-board and cratch. He whistled his appreciation, reached out to pick it up:

'May I?'

'Of course, Dad!'

He held it close, peering inside the hull to see how it was constructed, turning it over in his hands, the look of admiration in his eyes growing by the second:

'Where did this come from, Harry? It's beautifully built!'

'Jake made it himself.' His eyes met mine:

'He *did?*'

'Yes, Dad – I saw it weeks ago, before he'd finished it, but I didn't know he was going to give it to me, then.' He placed it carefully back down on the table, and continued to gaze at it for a while. His eyes lifted to mine again, and he held out his hands to me; as I took them in my own, he said:

'Harry – you remember what I said, that night after Jake had been here to dinner?' The memory caused me a twinge of pain; I nodded. He continued: 'Well, I owe you and Jake both a sincere apology. I was wrong about him; I know how much you like him, and this' he indicated the boat with a nod of his head 'tells me how much he must think of you, too. Do you understand what you've got, here?' I knew how much work had gone into the boat; I thought I could see what he was getting at:

'I think so, Dad.' He nodded:

'There are months, years even, of work in this. Patient, conscientious, painstaking work. You've been given a part of your friend's life, here, Harry, part of his soul. You understand?' I just nodded, humbled again by Jake's generosity; he went on: 'I misjudged him, Harry. I want you to tell him that, next time you see him, and apologise for me – will you do that?'

'Yes, Dad!'

'And tell him, if he wants to come here again, any time, I'll be pleased to welcome him, and I promise to treat him as a friend of yours deserves. I liked his father, when we met the other week, too.' Relieved and delighted, I let go of his hands and flung my arms around his neck; he laughed, and held me close.

* * *

Max and Nicky duly turned up, after Sunday Lunch – Mr Calvert, Nicky's Dad, ran a chemist's shop in North Oxford, and had been a friend of my mother's for many years. Both of my friends had brought me a present – the one which sticks in my memory now is the copy of Tom Rolt's book *Narrowboat,* which came from Nicky; I think my mother must have told Mr Calvert of my fascination with the canals. It still stands on my bookshelf today.

The grown-ups sat talking and sharing a bottle of wine in the cottage, while the three of us took the Spitfire out into the sunshine and flew it in turns around the pasture. We had a great time; it was wonderful to see my friends again, after so long, and yet I still felt as though something was not quite right – I had, I think, been looking forward to introducing them to Jake. I'd shown them the boat, which they both admired, asking me a lot about the canal and the boats which plied along it – I enjoyed playing the expert for once, even if I had to guess at one or two answers! But the day passed with a lot of fun and hilarity; the tea my mother had prepared was much appreciated by the adults as well as us kids, even if we were only allowed Coca-Cola in place of their sherry.

* * *

And then, as happened every year, the excitement of my birthday was followed by the rapid approach of the end of the school term. Now I was in senior school, we had to face the rigours of end-of-year exams, which to us in the first year were the source of much trepidation. In the end, they proved not to be so horrendous as we had been led to believe by some of the older boys – I don't think anyone disgraced themselves, although of course individual aptitudes showed through in the results. I scored well in maths and the sciences, as well as in art; Jake fell pretty much in the middle of the road, except that it came as no surprise to me when he came top of the year in woodwork. For the second year we were to be segregated by subject preference – those who showed a leaning toward the arts or languages in one stream, the scientists in the other. I knew where I would be, but Jake's position was more ambivalent; we shared a number of worried, inconclusive conversations, concerned at the possibility of finding ourselves separated but unable to influence the result.

The final selections were announced by Mr Atkinson, in his usual flippantly derogatory fashion, on the Monday of our last week. Read out in alphabetical order, each was greeted with muted cheers or groans, or a mixture of the two; the good news, as far as many were concerned, was that our potential bullies were to be parted: Peter Pocock, to give him his due, had a real flair for languages which put him unequivocally into the arts stream, while Tommy Smith was, like me, unquestionably a scientist. Then Snoop got to us, the last two names on the list:

'Mr Turner – since your skill at French and Latin resembles that of a circus seal, it has been decided that you stand more chance of a career if you stick to the sciences, despite your uncharacteristically high marks in art, although I have to say that your pictures show a certain pedantism which may suggest a future proficiency in *technical* drawing. Mr Woodrow – yours is a most difficult case, since you are pretty hopeless at everything. We have, however, decided that it may best serve your future interests, to say nothing of getting you out of *my* hair, if you too follow a scientific direction, at least until we know better.'

We turned to each other, grinning like Cheshire cats:

'Can't get away from me that easily!' I whispered, Jake replied:

'No – awful, isn't it?'

Chapter Nineteen

And so, at last, the last day of term. Seven weeks of holiday stretched out before us, their end too far in the distance to be recognised, even though we both knew in our hearts that that end would come around eventually, and all too soon, at that.

I have already said that that year of 1955 turned into a summer to be remembered – we rejoiced for practically all of our holiday under cloudless skies and warm sunshine. I spent several days in Oxford, with Max and Nicky; by arrangement, my father dropped me off in the morning before going back to Kidlington and his day at work, and then picked me up again on his way home in the evening. They were good days – our three-way friendship survived our gradually diverging lives, and continued to do so for a number of years. But, apart from those three or four days, and an occasional day out with my parents, when my father felt he could spare the time from the workshop, Jake and I spent the entire holiday, pretty well, in each other's company.

I had at last persuaded him to join us for a meal again, once the term had finished, and this time, the evening was an unbridled success. My mother abandoned many of the frills which she usually loved, serving us a simple but thoroughly marvellous dinner, and my father, trying, I suspect, to make up for his previous aloofness, made a tremendous fuss of my friend. After the meal, the two of them sat at the table, discussing at great length the details of how Jake had gone about building my boat, to the point that I began to feel rather left out. But then he let slip our ideas of going boating when we left school; I had not previously mentioned this to my father, but now he listened to our enthusiasm as we told him how we intended to go about things, nodding slowly, puffing at his cigarette. He said nothing to dampen our ardour, but I knew him well enough to tell from the look on his face that he harboured doubts about the practicality of our schemes – all he said, when our passion ran down, was that he'd rather hoped that I would join him in the engineering business, eventually, but:

'Your life is your own, Harry – you'll do what ever you decide, in the end, and have my support, come what may.' I got up, and gave him a hug, feeling Jake's smile warm on my back as I did so. Dad gave him a smile back across the table, and asked:

'Would you like to come and have a look around our works, Jake?'

'I'd love to, Mr Turner!'

'Right, then. What we'll do is this – you come here to dinner again soon, and bring some things with you, stay overnight. Then, in the morning, we'll all go in, and you can both spend the day there – if you're sure you want to?'

'I'm sure, Mr Turner!'

'That'd be great, Dad!'

So, the following week, Jake stopped in our spare

bedroom, and the two of us had a day in Kidlington. I could always find things to do there, and my old friend Henry Payne took Jake under his wing, showed him all of the machines and what each could do, let him try his hand on most of them. The natural ability with his hands which had evidenced itself in my boat showed through, so that by the end of the afternoon old Henry's eyes were sparkling with pleasure at the skill of his new acquaintance:

'Yew want a job when yew leaves school, young feller, yew come an' talk to me! Never mind Mr Turner' he chuckled at my father, standing beside us: 'Come an' see me, yew hear?'

'Yes, sir, Mr Payne! Thank you – and thank you for being so patient with me, today.' Henry ruffled his hair:

'Nao trouble, son, you're more than welcome – come agen, any time!'

Through the summer, it became a routine that, one day in the week, Jake would come over for dinner and stop the night. Once or twice more, we went to work with my father the following day; other times, we would head back together to the lock, and I would stay for the evening meal and usually overnight, or, more than once, for several nights in a row. Our days were spent partly in doing the usual round of chores to help Ernie Woodrow, or playing together in whatever way took out fancy. We would kick Jake's old football around in the field, go to the level-crossing and watch the trains, or indulge in any of the numerous, simple pleasures that appealed then to twelve-year-old kids.

In all of that glorious summer, I can hardly remember ever wearing my shirt. By the end of August, the two of us were both as brown as berries – Jake, with his outdoor lifestyle, had a natural, permanent tan, and despite my much paler colouring I was soon close on his heels. And it wasn't just on the bits that show, either – we would often take the short hike over the railway and up to the little tarn in the hills, and spend as much time as we could luxuriating in its cool waters, and then lying on the grass, talking idly of whatever came into our heads while the sun dried our bodies. Despite his best efforts, I never became a great swimmer; I tried, but I just couldn't quite get the knack of it. I could manage to thrash my way across the tarn and back without sinking, but I was never going to compete in the Olympics.

Every night when I stopped with him, Jake would take me with him out onto the lockside as dusk fell, as he had that first time. I came to understand, without either of us ever putting it into words, that this was his private time, normally, away from his father, sequestered with his own thoughts; and to understand, also, how much of a privilege it was to share it with him. He would invariably sit in the same place, on the balance beam of the top gate, facing North-West into the dying sunset. Sometimes we would talk, quietly; other times, we would just enjoy the silence and the beauty of the evening, watching in shared contentment as the stars slowly emerged into the darkening sky. It was at those times that the introspective side of his temperament showed itself – despite the school's judgement, I think he should have been an artist of some kind, a painter maybe, or a sculptor. Or even a writer.

During our days by the lock, I got to meet quite a few

more of the working boatmen and their families who were still, then, plying that part of the canal system. The only regular traffics were Joe Skinner, with his run from the Coventry coalfields to Banbury Co-op, and the Clayton's boats running from the gas works at Leamington Spa to Midland Tar Distillers in Banbury – I finally met Albert Beechey, their regular man on that trip, with his boats *Tay* and *Rea*. Thomas Clayton Ltd ran rather unusual boats, specially built to carry liquid cargoes – their holds were decked over with timber to form tanks, and the loads pumped in and out. Albert wasn't the most forthcoming of men I was to meet, but after we'd helped him a number of times, through the lock, and travelled with him to help at Bourton or Slat Mill as well, depending on which way he was going, he unbent enough to explain to me that they brought tar residues from Leamington, and then ran back to their base at Oldbury, in Birmingham, with what he called gas-water, to the chemical works there.

I met the Skinners quite regularly during that summer, and came to have a great affection for both the proud old boatman and his slim, bird-like wife. I think they quite liked me, too, but Joe especially never lost that air of reserve; I once heard someone describe him as a very private man, and I think that sums him up perfectly.

Other pairs would come by more irregularly; an occasional Barlow's boat, always immaculate in their dark green and oak-grain livery, or a pair from Willow Wren or the nationalised British Waterways fleet. I saw the Shines, Frank, Betty and Rachel, a number of times in those weeks, and became the recipient of many mugs of Rachel's strong, sweet tea as we rode with them between locks. And so many other families they would talk of - Littlemores, Hambridges, Granthams, Humphries, Boswells, Brays… Some I was to meet, others remained just names to me, even if Jake appeared to know them all. I had now got used to the way my friend's diction would suddenly switch back to his ancestral accent whenever he was talking to another boater; his self-conscious grin in my direction often giving away his own awareness of it.

And I began at last to understand that quiet warning Ernie Woodrow had given me when we first met – one or two among the men of the canal were less than friendly, seeming to accept me grudgingly, and only because I was a pal of Jake's. I plucked up the courage, one day, to ask Ernie why it was. He laid his pipe aside and looked at me:

'A lot of the folks on the bank won't 'ave nothin' ter do wi' the boatees, 'Arry – call 'em Gypsies, or dirty Bargees. Yeh can 'ardly blame the boaters if they treat *them* the same way, can yeh? It's not really meant personal, but they're suspicious of anyone outside our own world, yeh see. Don't take it amiss – they'll most of 'em be 'appy once they get ter know yeh.'

Chapter Twenty

Whenever the opportunity arose, we would cross-examine any passing boater about our own plans, asking how they saw the future of the canals and the carrying trade. Some were encouraging, although many of them told us to make the best of it while we could, believing that the end of the business would come eventually; a few told us bluntly to forget it, that by the time we were old enough to have our own boats the jobs would be gone. But, as if to lift our spirits, into this gloom came a ray of hope – a ray called Tom Foxon.

Tom was the man Ernie had mentioned, who had secured a contract to supply coal by boat to Morrell's Brewery. He had acquired an old wooden motor boat, built in the thirties for the Grand Union company, and renamed it the *New Hope.* He ran it as a single motor, with no butty; we met him several times, and found his drive and enthusiasm for the job to be as great as our own. And he had an unshakeable belief that trade could be brought back to the canal, if people had the conviction to go for it. The sight of Tom's cheerful face, of the approaching fore-end of the *New Hope,* and the steady thud-thud-thud-thud-thud of its two-cylinder engine, was guaranteed to buck us up every time. A couple of times, at a nod from his father, Jake and I rode with him all the way to Banbury, helping with the locks and the occasional lift-bridge, and then struck out for the three-mile walk back. He was good company, and his keenness served to bolster our own; and he would let us take a turn at the tiller, as well!

At first, I was terrified at the idea of steering seventy feet of boat; Jake, of course, had no qualms about it, having taken a hand with his father's years before, at the tender age of seven, standing on an orange box to see over the cabin. But it was not as difficult as I expected; soon, I found myself thoroughly enjoying the experience, enthralled at the very idea of having some forty tons of boat under my command. The *New Hope* was so easy to handle, almost seeming to find her own way around the twists and turns of the channel, and far more responsive under my hands than I had expected; and Tom was so trusting, wandering off to check the engine, polish the brasses, or brew a pot of tea, leaving the two of us in sole charge of his livelihood. I hated having to give it back to him, on the approach to a lock!

* * *

The August bank holiday then fell on the first weekend of the month, not the last as it does today; and, as Ernie Woodrow had heard, on that particular bank holiday the Inland Waterways Association, an enthusiast group dedicated to the preservation of the canals, had organised a big rally at Banbury to protest again at the proposals to close the length from there to Oxford.

I was at Burdon Lock with Jake on the Friday, when

a lot of boats were passing through on their way there. Most were pleasure craft of one sort or another – some of them old working boats, converted or cut down to a smaller size, others modern wood or fibreglass cabin-cruisers, even a few old ships' lifeboats with rough cabins tacked onto them. But then, among them appeared a pair, running empty, their fore-ends high out of the water as if proud of their professional status among their lesser brethren.

I had never seen boats so immaculately turned out – all the working boatmen and their wives kept their boats clean and shining, but these were gleaming with new paint and brasses which shone like gold in the sun. We set to with a will to work them through the lock, in company with the boatman, who looked vaguely familiar although I didn't think we'd met before. His first words to Jake confirmed that:

'Good to see yeh, Jake – Oo's yer pal?'

'That's 'Arry, Jack – 'E's me mate from school.'

'Oh – Ah! Good teh meet yer, 'Arry!'

'Nice to meet you, sir!'

'Not sir – Jack, Jack Skinner. Thanks fer yer 'elp, boys!' He grinned at us; we smiled back and went on working, pulling the paddles to drop his spotless boat in the lock. Was he related to Old Joe Skinner, I wondered, was that why I'd thought he looked familiar? I'd learnt by now that many of the boating families were inter-related, by blood or marriage. After they had gone on their way, with a cheery wave from his wife as she settled into the butty's hatches, Jake confirmed my suspicion:

'Jack's old Joe's nephew. His missus is called Rose too – confusing, ain't it?'

'Rather!'

We'd learnt, as they passed through, that they had been sent to the rally by their boss, Mr Morton, to represent Willow Wren – hence the immaculate turn-out of the boats, *Redshank* and *Greenshank*.

Later that same day, another Willow Wren pair appeared – Frank, Betty and Rachel Shine, with their *Greylag* and *Grebe*. Their boats, in contrast, were loaded, and, although as smart as always, not so spectacularly polished as Jack Skinner's pair. They were carrying a regular load for Banbury and had managed to time their trip to coincide with the rally:

'Whoy doon't the two o' yeh coom n' see us oover the weekend, boys?' Frank suggested. We looked at each other:

'Yeah – mebbe we could...' Jake sounded eager.

'I'm supposed to go and see my friends in Oxford, tomorrow' I reminded him.

'Oh, yeah – how 'bout Sunday? Come over to our house, and we could walk into town!'

'Yeah – okay, why not?' I was going out for the day with my parents on the holiday Monday, so that idea suited me well. The thought of a three-mile hike each way no longer phased me as it might have done a few months before – I was fitter than I think I had ever been in my life, by then. I nodded: 'We'll see you there, Frank!'

* * *

We spent a wonderful day at the rally, wandering around all the boats in the sunshine – the glorious weather of that summer still showed no sign of ending. We chatted with Jack and Rose Skinner, went along on one of trips they were running up through our own territory to Cropredy and back, working the locks for them – we just took the motor boat, so it didn't take as long to go there and back as might be expected. *Redshank* was still as clean and bright as a new pin, and Jack had a huge Union flag hung from the tiller. The next little while, we sat drinking tea and chatting with Rachel in her butty cabin, while Frank and Betty stood outside talking to the crowds of visitors 'doin' our bit fer the cut', as Frank put it.

That night, after walking to the lock, all the way into Banbury and back, and then home again, I was deliciously exhausted, and fell into bed before nine without protest, to my mother's surprise. After a night's sleep in which I don't recall waking once, my father took us to Hampshire the following day, to see the magnificent motor museum at Beaulieu.

On the Tuesday, I was back at the lock again with Jake – we'd guessed that many of the boats from the rally would be heading for home then, and so it proved! We had a great day, helping all and sundry through, and earning quite a few shillings from the private boaters for our efforts. We saw Jack and Rose Skinner again, headed back to load at Griff Colliery – Jack told us that he was to run a trial load down to Oxford, for Morrell's, to see how easy it was to get a loaded pair all the way through; we said we'd look out for them. We didn't see the Shines that day, but as Jake said, they'd probably have been unloading.

It was near the end of the month when Jack and Rose came through with their load:

'Forty-seven 'n a 'alf ton we got on! Soom o' the bridge-'oles down by h'Oxford'll be a bit sticky, boot we'll get there, you see if we doon't!' And they did.

And so passed the best summer of my life. But, as the saying goes, all good things must come to an end...

Chapter Twenty-One

The last weekend of the holiday, and the fine weather had broken at last. I trod the familiar path from the village to Burdon Lock through a warm but steady rain, looking forward as ever to another day in the company of my soulmate. I think by then both of us were assuming that, come what may in terms of marriages and children, studies and careers, whether on the cut or elsewhere, our futures would be inextricably joined.

Having had two willing helpers all through the summer, Ernie Woodrow was running short of tasks to give us. We spent that morning weeding the vegetable garden again, and pulling up a few carrots and potatoes for their Sunday dinner – the stew for that night was already burbling quietly to itself in the oven. After lunch, Jake and I wandered along the towpath to Burdon Bridge, where the bridleway crossed, and sat on the parapet for a while, kicking our heels on the brickwork and talking about our impending return to school, and the visit to St Giles' Fair in Oxford which we had to look forward to on the Monday. The rain had stopped now, although the skies were still grey and overcast.

By local tradition, term began on the Wednesday – Monday and Tuesday were the days when the fair came to the city. I had been every year, for as long as I could remember, but Jake had never seen it – my father had offered to take us both into town that Monday, and leave us with the Calverts. The meeting between my two old friends and my new companion was finally going to happen; I was torn by the prospect, eager to show Jake off to Max and Nicky, but at the same time a little wary of their reaction to him: Like me, they came from what I might now describe as comfortable, middle-class families, and I think I harboured a certain concern that, like the Smiths of this world, they wouldn't take to the penniless lock-keeper's son.

Our shared reverie was eventually disturbed by a faint tug-tug-tug-tug-tug from the North, and a short, sharp blast on the old bugle which Frank Shine kept to hand to signal his approach. We looked around, to see the pair working through Slat Mill Lock in the distance:

'Come on, we'll 'ave Burdon ready for 'em!' Jake jumped to the ground, and we set off back to the lock. By the time they appeared through the distant bridge, we had the top gates open; Frank slid the motor in, casting off his towline as he did so, while Betty brought the butty to rest above the lock. We whistled him through, closing the bottom gates behind the boat as Bet and Rachel whipped up the top paddles again. With the lock refilled, Bet swung the gate, and Jake and I took the towline and began to haul the butty in; Rachel had disappeared into the cabin to put the kettle on for out traditional mug of tea while we rode down to Bourton with them.

Even a loaded butty quickly picks up speed, hauled by two eager youngsters like us. Leaving Jake still pulling, I dropped the rope and ran toward the far end of the lock ready to raise the paddle, stooping to pick up my windlass as I ran. But as I bent down, my foot slipped on the wet grass. Completely unbalanced, I tried to save myself…

The shock of the water as I toppled over the edge threw me into a panic. It wasn't that I'd fallen in – as I've said, I could swim, if not particularly strongly or elegantly – but rather the closeness of the boat, the awareness of its remorseless approach, the knowledge that thirty-plus tons, once in motion, doesn't stop again terribly easily. I went under, fought my way back to the surface, thrashing about blindly in my terror, began to go down again, scrabbling at the coping stones which lined the chamber…

And then strong hands grabbed me by the waist, launched me into the air. The last thing I saw as I passed out was Frank Shine, towering over me on the lockside; I felt him seize my wrists, lift me bodily from the water as those other hands thrust from below, now pushing on my rump…

I must have been unconscious for quite a few minutes. When I came to, it was to see Frank bending over me, a look of relief on his face as I opened my eyes:

'Thank God! You all roight, boy?' I coughed up some of the water I'd swallowed:

'I think so – thank you!' He nodded:

'You jus' loy still, then, take it easy.' My thoughts turned to Jake – in my shame and distress, I wanted my friend; and it must have been him who had been behind me, lifting me out of the lock – where was he?

'Jake…' Pain flashed across Frank's face, but he told me:

'Don't worry 'bout 'im, for now – you loy there 'n get oover it.' I tried to raise my head, puzzled at his absence, looked around: The boat was still in the full lock, and Ernie Woodrow was sitting on the gunwale, his feet braced on the lockside, elbow on one knee, his face in his hand. A few feet away, Betty was kneeling on the ground, her own hands resting on the knees of her full skirt, her head bowed, an air of hopelessness about her posture.

Beside her, my friend lay on his back. He wasn't moving; he must have been hurt – but she was doing nothing to help him…!

'Jake? What's wrong? *Jake!*'

Chapter Twenty-Two

We buried my best friend in the village churchyard. His tombstone stands there still; I go to it occasionally, pull up the weeds which begin to encroach on it, keep the stone itself as clean as I can, cut the grass around it:

JACOB WOODROW
Beloved Son of Ernest
September 1942 - September 1955
May You Boat
The Waterways of Heaven
Forever

* * *

On the lockside, I had struggled to go to him. I fought off Frank Shine, as he tried to restrain me, crawled across the grass when I found that my damaged ankle wouldn't support me. I knelt over him, wiped away the trickle of blood which had escaped from his nostril, unable to accept or believe what I knew; I slipped my arm under his neck, lifted him into my arms, and then laid him gently down again, easing myself down beside him, holding him close.

They told me later that I lay with him for almost two hours, trying to warm him with my body, trying to somehow share my life with him, to bring him back. Even when the ambulancemen, summoned from the telephone in our house by Rachel after a frantic dash across the fields, arrived with a stretcher tucked under their arms, I refused to let them touch him – taking one look, they let me be, knowing that all of their skill and training was to be of no avail this time. My mother was there – she had followed Rachel back, after quickly calling my father to tell him what had happened. She sat beside me, although I wasn't aware of her presence; the two boatwomen had taken Ernie into their cabin and were doing their best to look after him.

It was my father, rushing to me after leaving Henry Payne in charge at work, who finally got me to relinquish my possession of Jake's body, and gently led me into the lock-cottage, where my mother persuaded me to take some of the tea she'd been making on and off for the last hour. Between them, they got me home, after the ambulancemen had taken Jake away, and Ernie had emerged from the butty cabin and encircled me in his one arm; I hadn't been able to speak to him, choking into silence as I tried to express my pain and horror; he had just held me, the tears still streaming down his face, but at last, his voice strangled with emotion, he said:

'Wasn't your fault, 'Arry. You moostn't blame yourself, boy. Now goo on 'ome – Oi'll be okay, Frank 'n Betty'll stay 'n look after me.'

'I'm… so sorry, Mr Woodrow…' I finally got out. He gave my shoulders a squeeze and turned away, his head bowed.

* * *

We buried him on the following Saturday, the day which should have been his thirteenth birthday. Pretty well all the village was there – not, I suspect, out of any great love of the 'dirty boatees', but because the story of what had happened had gone around, and their fascination for such a tale of tragic heroism brought them out.

A good number of boaters were there, all dressed in their best. Frank, Betty and Rachel, of course, supporting Ernie throughout the ceremony; at the graveside, when it was all over, he held me close, mumbled hoarsely:

'Thank you fer bein' a good friend to my boy, 'Arry...'
I felt he wanted to say more, but neither he nor I could get any words out. Frank took my hands in his, told me how sad he was that I'd lost my friend; Betty swept me into her arms, tears in her eyes, practically smothering me in her sympathy and her more-than-ample bosom; Rachel, too gave me a prolonged hug, told me I would always be welcome on their boats, to be sure to keep in touch.

Albert and Suey Beechey were there, their boats tied up at the lock along with the *New Hope*, their trip and Tom's interrupted to show their respect for Ernie and his son; and I saw Joe and Rose Skinner, standing almost self-consciously at the back. When he came up to me, took me by the hand, I was touched by the light of sadness in Joe's eyes:

''E was a good lad, young Jake – We'll all miss 'im.'
Rose, too threatened to stifle me with her emotional embrace.

Everyone there seemed to want to talk to me. I soon found myself tiring of the continual expressions of sympathy and condolence, desperately wanting to get away, to be on my own. And then, I found myself confronted with Tommy Smith.

I hadn't been to school, although term had been in for two days, now. Mr Atkinson had come, and Mr Wanstone; I was pleased that they had had enough respect for my friend to be there. But to see *him*, of all my fellow-pupils… Smith came over to me, a wary look in his eyes:

'Turner? I'm… sorry, really sorry.'

'What are *you* doing here?' I was angry, thinking he had come to cause trouble, to make one of his snide remarks.

'I'm *sorry,* please… I heard what happened, *all* about it – I've never heard of anything so brave. That makes him a hero, in my book, okay? I'm sorry, for all the times we got at him, and, and… Forgive me?' My anger was beginning to subside, but I couldn't resist snapping back:

'*He* can't forgive you *now,* can he?' He hung his head, and went to turn away; but then he looked up, and I saw the reality of the remorse in his face:

'I deserve that, I know. But I *am* sorry, whether you believe it or not!' He turned back to me, held out a hand: 'Truce, at least?' I stared at him for a moment, knowing the truth of his feelings, seeing in his eyes what it had cost him in self-respect to admit them. I took his hand in mine, shaking my head:

'No truce. Friends, maybe?' He smiled, shook my hand firmly:

'Friends, Harry.'

* * *

Everyone came back to our house – Ernie could hardly have accommodated them all at the lock, even if they wanted to trek out there. My mother had laid on a buffet, and people circulated, drinking wine or tea, talking in hushed tones all the while. I found myself still the centre of attention, or one of them, sharing the limelight with Jake's father; I soon wanted nothing more than to get out of there, to get away from all the well-meant words, all the stifling sympathy, to be alone with my thoughts for a while.

Anticlimax was already setting in – I knew the difficult part was about to begin, the trying to go on with my life without my friend, the trying to accept that never again would we sit and watch the trains go by, never again go skinny-dipping in the tarn, never again sit and listen to his father's memories of his boating days, never again talk and plan our future on the canal, a future which now had no existence… Never again would we laugh together; never again would we sit by the lock in the starlight, sharing that warm silence…

Never again…

Drowning in my own sorrow, I fought my way to the front door and ran from the house.

Chapter Twenty-Three

With nowhere else to go, I found myself back by the village green, leaning on the low stone wall of the churchyard, staring over the jumbled headstones towards the distant flower-covered pile of soil which lay next to the grave. I clambered over the wall and sat on its rough top, unaware of the sharp stones digging into my anatomy, uncaring that the dirt and lichens were soiling my best suit.

Time passed; I no longer remember the thoughts which echoed hollowly through my head – I think I was trying *not* to think at all, because all the thoughts I had were too painful to be held. But at least I was away from all the faces and the voices in our house, safe from their well-intentioned but uncomprehending words, their sad, sympathetic smiles…

My unseeing eyes at last registered the presence of another figure, walking across the graveyard from behind the church, a spade slung casually over its shoulder. I knew Terry Earlham – he had a small farm just outside the village, to the South. A great bear of a man, well over six feet and built like an ox, someone had told me once that he was also the village's gravedigger; probably on one of the nights when we had seen him in the pub, where I sat with my lemonade and a bag of crisps while my parents enjoyed a quiet drink, as they liked to do on occasions. Not that you could have a quiet drink if Terry was there – well-read and well-educated, he enjoyed a debate on any subject for its own sake, the more vehement the better. I sometimes wondered if, when roused, his views could be heard across the county – he had a deep and powerful voice which could make the floor vibrate under your feet.

Now, I watched him carefully remove the mound of flowers and wreaths, laying them gently to one side, and roll away the tarpaulin which had covered the earth itself. He picked up the spade, and stood looking down into the grave, his head bowed; I knew without needing to be told that he was praying, praying for the soul of my friend.

I got up, and walked over to stand beside him; he gave a start, and turned to look down on me:

'God, boy, you'll give me a heart attack, creeping up like that!'

'Sorry, Mr Earlham.' I hung my head; he reached down, lifted my chin with his big paw:

'Harry Turner – I'm sorry, I didn't realise it was you, son.' His foghorn voice was suddenly soft, gentle with compassion.

'It's all right.' He let go, but stood gazing down at me:

'Should you be here, Harry?' I shrugged:

'Maybe not – but I had to get out of *there* – everyone's at our house, and I couldn't stand it any longer!' He nodded:

'I know, son. But – I've got a job to do, now. You understand?' And then I knew what I had to do, what I *needed* to do:

'Can *I*, Mr Earlham? Please?' He stared at me, uncertain, but then he said:

'If you want to, son, if you're sure – you start, then I'll finish off, shall I?' I think he was wondering if I could manage, if I had the strength or the stamina, but I nodded. He handed me the spade, turned me, stood behind me, almost cradling me in his massive arms as he showed me how to swing the blade into the heaped-up earth, to lift and turn it, and to up-end it over the hole where Jake's coffin lay indecently uncovered below us. After the first few strokes, he left me to it, and went a few steps away to sit on the raised bench of a huge old sarcophagus in the next row of graves.

He watched me, slowly taking out a battered pipe, filling it, lighting it, and puffing thoughtfully as I worked. It was another overcast day, grey and dull, but the air was still warm and muggy; after a few minutes, I paused to throw off my jacket, unknot my tie. He stood up, thinking perhaps that I had had enough, but settled back to his perch as I took up the spade again. Before long I had my shirt undone to the waist, sweating with my exertions; but I didn't, couldn't, give up. The only idea in my head was that this was the last service I would ever perform for my friend in this life – I worked on, until most of the earth lay back in the hole from which it had come, until the remaining pile was little more than a layer over the grass. At last, as I stumbled in my fatigue, Terry Earlham stood up and put his arm around my shoulders:

'You've done enough, son, I'll finish the job off now. You go and sit down for a while.' I gave him the spade, and sat reluctantly on the old tomb while he laid the last few shovelfuls of soil in place, smoothed the surface with the flat of the blade. Then he turned to me:

'I think we'd better get you home, Harry. Your folks'll be wondering where you are.'

'Oh, Harry, where on earth have you been?' My mother's voice was frightened rather than angry. She stared at the state of me, my jacket and tie slung over one arm, my shirt ragged and dirty, my trousers ruined, my once-shiny shoes caked in mud, and a streak of earth on my face where I'd wiped my brow with a muddy forearm.

'I'm sorry, Mrs Turner – he's been with me. I should have sent him home earlier…'

'But he wouldn't come! I know my son, Mr Earlham. Thank you for looking after him, and bringing him back now. Come in, please, take a drink with us before you go?'

'Thank you, Ma'am, but no. I'd best get home – Jean will be waiting on me for dinner, and I'm late already.'

'If you're sure, then? Thank you again.' He turned with a wave of his hand, a nod of his shaggy head in my direction; the look in his eyes held respect as well as sympathy as he smiled at me.

'Upstairs, Harry, in the bath with you!' As my mother propelled me gently towards the stairs, my father emerged from the dining-room, his expression changing to one of surprise as he caught sight of me:

'Harry…?'

'I've been helping Mr Earlham, Dad.'

'The gravedigger…' He came over to me, took me in his arms and held me close: 'I'm so sorry, son.' His voice was barely audible; then he pushed me away: 'Look at the mess you've made of my suit! Up in the bath with you, now!' His jocular words were spoken with softness and sympathy, his smile belying their meaning, but I couldn't echo it however hard I tried.

I ate little that night, and slept even less. I tossed and turned, memories and fears competing for my attention, the poignancy of the past fighting with the hopelessness of the future. Through all the sadness and sympathy I had endured through the last week, what no-one seemed to understand was that it was *all my fault!* If I hadn't fallen in the lock, if I hadn't been *running* on the wet grass, if I hadn't been so *stupid...*

I must have dozed from time to time, but by half past six the next morning, I had had enough of my comfortless bed. I crawled out into the early morning light, dressed in whatever clothes came to hand, and stumbled downstairs to the kitchen. Searching through the cupboards for one of the mugs we usually had cocoa in before bed, during the winter, I made myself some strong, sweet, Ernie Woodrow-style tea, and sat at the table sipping at it, wondering what to do with myself. Finding no answer, I dropped the empty mug into the sink, slipped on the old coat I would usually wear for the walk across the fields to the lock, and let myself quietly out of the front door.

Wandering without reason or direction, I found myself again on the village green, beside the stone wall of the churchyard; again, I clambered over, sat looking out over the accumulated bereavement of some centuries to my own present sorrow. Sunday had dawned to another grey overcast; the weather suited my mood, as grief and guilt chased each other around in my brain. I kept no count of time; its passage seemed irrelevant, even if the chiming of the steeple clock interrupted my reverie at intervals.

* * *

'Back again, Harry?' Suddenly, I wasn't alone. Terry Earlham stepped over the low wall, took a seat beside me. He looked down at me for a moment, then set about carefully filling his pipe, lighting it, tamping down the tobacco, relighting it, until he was satisfied, and a cloud of aromatic smoke began to drift around his head. I didn't resent his presence; I felt a camaraderie in his silence which somehow strengthened me. Between puffs, he spoke again:

'You know, Harry, I've helped to bury a lot of 'em, over the years. Young 'uns as well as old 'uns, sometimes. And one thing I've learnt – wherever they are, Harry, they're not here. If they all stopped here, it would be pretty crowded by now, wouldn't it?' His macabre humour might seem out of place, stated baldly like that, but it put the first smile on my face for over a week. He saw it, and smiled back:

'I didn't know him. He must have been pretty special, to inspire loyalty like yours, young man. But – take my word for it, boy, wherever he is, he isn't here…' He looked up in surprise as I leapt to my feet:

'Thank you, Mr Earlham!' I scrambled over the wall and set off down the lane, leaving him gazing after me, shaking his head at the unpredictability of youth.

Chapter Twenty-Three

Terry Earlham might not have known where Jake would be, but I did. There was only one place where his spirit would want to linger…

I hurried past our front door, almost at a run, past Manor Farm, and onto the bridleway behind the barn. I don't know what I expected – I was too sensible to think I might find him there in any way I could see or touch, but still, that was his place, his world, as he'd told me so often, and if he was anywhere at all, that would be where. I think, as much as anything, I wanted be able to say sorry to him, rather as Tommy Smith had felt the need to say sorry to me; and there, in the place he had loved, the place where he had lived and died, I might, perhaps, be able to do that…

But as I strode along the all-too-familiar way, I began to feel doubts assail me. What *I* wanted was one thing – but what about his father? What about Ernie Woodrow – would he want to see *me?* I was the reason his son was dead; and the sight of me might be too much of a reminder of what he had lost. He would probably send me away, angry at my presumption in daring to go back there. Time and again, I almost gave up, turned back, afraid to face him, afraid to face *myself,* perhaps. But somehow, something kept me pressing on, one foot in front of the other, through the fine mist of rain which had begun to fall, until I found the red-brick of the cottage looming out of the greyness before me.

There was no sign of life, the drab stillness a dramatic contrast with the sight of the cheery one-armed lock-keeper bustling in the yard, waving his habitual greeting, which I had become used to. I was grateful for that - I supposed he would be closeted within, wrapped up in his grief. I didn't go to the door – I walked carefully through the garden, where the two of us had happily pulled weeds so often, stepped out onto the lockside, hoping that he wouldn't see me, at least, not yet…

I stood for a moment, the sadness boring into my heart; then I walked slowly along, to the top gate. I stepped over the balance beam, sat down on its damp surface, uncaring about the wetness which quickly penetrated my trousers.

This was his place. I bowed my head, saying my silent prayer of apology, making my unspoken farewell to the companion whose friendship had brought me so much happiness, whose simple presence in my life had meant so much, whose loyalty had saved my life, at the end of his own.

It was as silent then as on the unnumbered evenings when we had sat out there together, contemplating our shared future under the companionable light of the stars. But the quiet which then had been warm and comfortable was now oppressive, agonising, echoing to me ever and again that that future, those dreams and schemes, would never be, that it was all over. Two words echoed unceasingly in my mind:

Never again…

Around me, the grey morning wept, crying for my loneliness.

Uncounted time passed. And suddenly, I found, for the second time that day, that I was not alone. Ernie Woodrow stepped around the balance beam, sat beside me:

'Saw yeh coom, a whoile agoo, 'Arry. 'Ow are yeh, boy?'

'Mr Woodrow…'

'Oi know, boy.'

I felt his arm slip around my shoulders – we sat, unspeaking, for an age.

'Your friendship was 'is whole loife, 'Arry. Oi owe yeh so much fer that.' I looked up as he finally broke the silence:

'But…'

'Hush, boy! Oi know what yer feelin'. If 'e 'ad ter go now, 'e couldn't 'ave doied a better way – 'e'd tell yeh so 'imself, if 'e could.'

'But if…'

'*If,* 'Arry? What's that mean, eh? It's up to you, now. Grow up strong and straight, make the best of yerself, be a *good* man, and what 'e gave you will 'ave been worth it.'

I could only nod, as the tears rose to my eyes again; he held me close as I buried my face in his shoulder. I felt his body shaking quietly, and knew that he was crying too.

An eternity later, he eased me to my feet:

'Coom on insoide, boy. Oi'll put the kettle on.'

Epilogue

I come out here every night.

It's so beautiful – whatever the weather, whatever the season. I like to sit here, on my own, on the lock-gate as evening turns slowly into night, and the world falls silent around me. Just the gentle murmur of water, chucking as it creeps past the quoins of the gate and trickles into the lock, making the quiet of twilight that much more intense by its unobtrusive presence.

My aloneness is of my own choosing.

I know that I have only to say the word, to drop the slightest of hints, to be welcomed into the arms of my family, to be with my son and his lovely wife, enjoying the robust, carefree vitality of their two boys, or with one of my girls. Jenny, so full of quiet pride as her own daughter prepares to present me with my first great-grandson, this side of Christmas, or Sarah, my youngest, the high-flyer, in her elegant home with her fellow-lawyer husband.

But, at this time of the day, in this place, I choose to be alone.

I have had a full life – but, although that echoing emptiness from my childhood has diminished in proportion, it is still there. Anything less would be an injustice, a disloyalty to Jake, and the time we had together; now, I can look back at it, and remember. 'What if' is a purposeless expression – and yet, it repeats and repeats in my mind as I gaze at the stars glittering in the still, dark water, as I gaze towards a distant horizon where I can see, inexorable if indeterminate, the end of my own life approaching.

This never was my place.

From the beginning, it was *his* place; even if, for so short a time, he was happy to allow me to share it with him, it can never be mine. I still remember nights like this, sitting here with him, gazing out along the Burdon Straight to where the canal disappears at last under the distant bridge. I remember watching, as I do tonight, in silent wonder, as the sky, reflected in the polished mirror of the water, darkened gradually from tones of rose and amber through shades of blue into the black of night, and each star slowly emerged into full view, like a shy child creeping out from behind a door to stare at a stranger.

So many years.

Almost fifty of them, since that awful day. And it took so many years, before I found any kind of peace. Guilt and grief were my suppressed companions for so long, if only because I knew that *he* had known: He must have realised, as he dived into the water intent on saving me from my own stupidity, that his own chances of getting out again in time were infinitesimal. But, we both knew that I would have done the same for him; that was how our friendship worked. Closer than brothers could ever be – it is the greatest privilege of my life to have known friendship of that kind, and its greatest sadness to have lost it so soon. But how often, in those years, did I wish that it could have been so, that he could have lived in my stead?

It was Mary, my beautiful, gentle, loving Mary, who finally made me see just how great his gift to me had been, made me learn to accept it with grace. I never forgot those words of Ernie's, either, never lost the sense of living a part of my life in trust – if I have made a mark on the world, it is as much his mark as it is mine.

So now, I sit here, alone, as twilight gathers, as the autumn bats begin to fly, swooping, skimming low over the water to take their evening feast. And I wonder: If he had not intervened, if he had left that fateful day to what I *know* was its pre-ordained course, would his children and grandchildren now, somehow, be occupying the spaces left in the world by the absence of mine?

But most of all, I wonder – would *he* be sitting here now, in the silent starlight, wondering, and remembering...?

Also from SGM Publishing:

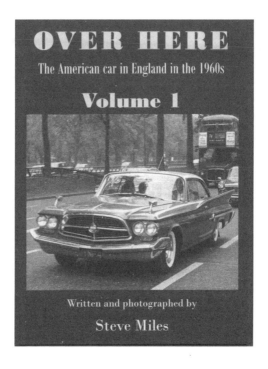

Published by SGM at the end of 2004, this exciting new title may be ordered from any good bookshop.

Just ask for
Over Here by Steve Miles   ISBN 0-9545624-4-5
published by SGM Publishing.

Tel: 07792 497116
www.sgmpublishing.co.uk